Sv

Jeremy Megargee

SWEET TREATS FIRST EDITION

ISBN-13: 978-1508917045

ISBN-10: 1508917043

www.facebook.com/JMHorrorFiction

Cover design by MNS Art Studio

For my Grandpa, a man who loved the mountains and valleys that he called home. He always told the best stories...

"Monsters are real, and ghosts are real too. They live inside us, and sometimes, they win."

- Stephen King

Prologue

It started slow.

It was like a quiet trickle from a rusted tap, nothing but a barely seen shadow passing over the little town of Greyfield. Life was simple in that humble slice of West Virginia. Mostly blue collar folk toiling to keep families afloat doing whatever they could. It was an old town full of old blood and everyone knew everyone. There were undoubtedly secrets behind many of the town's locked doors, but privacy was something to be respected here. A man's troubles were his own.

Children were starting to vanish in Greyfield. At first the townsfolk blamed the Potomac River (which cuts directly through the town center) but as time went on, it became apparent that not all of these kids were playing too close to the river's edge and being swept away by the strong currents. Something much darker was happening here.

Missing posters littered the bulletin board in the post office and they could be seen flapping in the wind on almost every electrical pole in town. Parents took to holding their children's hands a little too tightly, watching like hawks as the school buses arrived and departed. There was a mistrustful haze settling over Greyfield. Some families packed up and moved to either Morgantown or Rust Valley, the closest havens to escape the spreading malignance of fear.

The Greyfield Police Department kept coming up empty. They'd find little clues, the occasional scrap of clothing or a discarded plastic lunchbox. The trail always ran cold, though. They weren't sure if they were dealing with multiple individuals or a solitary fox in the town's henhouse. Red and blue lights flashed late into the night as they cruised along deserted streets. The police officers survived on copious amounts of coffee and pure dogged hope, but night after night, the patrols proved fruitless.

The children kept disappearing.

The culprit remained, unidentified and unchained.

Greyfield was in the grip of dread.

Small towns suffer quietly, but sometimes they suffer deepest of all.

1

Jack

I was chasing toads when he got me.

Out on the north end of town there are some bogs behind an old abandoned box factory. They're the result of runoff from the Potomac, the river creating these little pools of fetid water. They're so stinky that they make me curl my nostrils when I'm around them, but they're the absolute best place to catch toads in Greyfield.

There's this one particular willow tree that is grown up into the shattered brickwork of the old factory. The roots almost remind me of tentacles coming up from underground to pull down sections of the wall. The tree kind of leans out over the bog and toads love the damp little area below the roots, the water sloshing up against a tiny circle of mud.

I can climb my way around the trunk and venture out on the biggest root, using my hands and knees to crawl out and peek underneath into that special spot. It's a beautiful evening and fireflies are just starting to flutter through the air. I've gotta be quick because if I'm not back before dark then mom will pitch a fit.

I see my own reflection in the murky water. Dirty blonde hair, bright blue eyes, and a mouth prone to sarcastic smirks. I love making my friends laugh and that smirk is like my trademark, it always follows a particularly good vulgar joke. My dream is to one day make it big as a stand-up comedian. I guess it's good for a twelve year old kid to have dreams.

My attention is immediately diverted from my own reflection when I catch sight of the whopper hiding away down in my special spot. She's one of the biggest American toads I've ever seen. I can tell it's a female because she has a light colored throat as opposed to a darker colored one. If I can negotiate this big momma into my critter keeper then this evening will be a complete success.

I have a seventy five gallon terrarium at home for my pet toads and I absolutely love watching them. The little amphibians have so much personality and they always put on one hell of a show when I drop a few crickets or mealworms into their home. I just planted my new terrarium and put in a little waterfall, so if I manage to catch her, she'll be bound for toad heaven.

I'm already reaching quietly for the plastic critter keeper. Stealth is key when it comes to the fine art of toad catching, the slightest jerky movement could cause her to leap forward into the bog water and vanish into the stinky depths.

I'm vaguely aware of a sound behind me but I barely pay attention to it because I'm so focused on getting this prize toad. It sounds like metal jangling against metal on a tool belt. My concentration is broken by heavy footsteps literally just a few feet away from me. I'm still splayed on my belly across the roots of the tree and I have to crane my neck around to look up.

The sun is starting to set on the horizon and it glints directly into my eyes, turning the figure into something that looks like a massive black hole. I can tell that the man is incredibly large, both tall and fat. I can make out a greasy ponytail but not much of the man's features due to the glare.

He hooks a hand into his belt and just looks at me for a minute. I hear a grotesque sucking sound and I realize he just removed a lollipop from his mouth. It's green apple flavored, held there in one meaty fist as he stares down at me.

I bring one hand up to try and shield my eyes against the sun.

"Hello?"

That's all I manage before a boot crunches down against the plastic of my critter keeper. It shatters...and then a hand is yanking at my hair, digging directly down into the roots. Another meaty hand moves down to the tool belt and something hard hits me on the temple.

I'm stunned and about to flop into the bog water before the hand hauls up on my hair again and slings me over a mountainous shoulder. I blink my eyes and try hard to stay awake but I feel terribly tired. I can see the fireflies but then they start to fade, the little lights of them winking out. My temple feels wet and sticky.

Finally I succumb to that tired feeling, my body swaying from side to side as the man carries me through the abandoned box factory.

I never did get that toad.

2

Jack

The next few days passed in putrid monotony. I woke up chained to a busted radiator in a drab little room with a cracked concrete floor. My head ached constantly and I could barely get one of my eyes to open up all the way. I tried to yank and pull at the chain but there was absolutely no give. It was horribly hot in this room, my dirty clothes saturated with sweat.

He came to visit every night. He hit me, he cut me, and he burned me.

He liked to use wrenches to hit me. They left deep bruises that changed color multiple times, turning first yellow and then a sallow purple. The colors reminded me of a kaleidoscope.

Sometimes he'd use just his meaty fists to pound me into submission. His knuckles would bite into me over and over again. There was a ring on his right hand, a gaudy piece of costume jewelry overtopped with a chipped turquoise stone. After the third day that ring knocked two of my front teeth out and broke one of my canines in half.

Attempting to fight him was useless; he outweighed me by over three hundred pounds or so. He was obese, a bulbous gut spilling out overtop a pair of soiled white briefs. That's all he ever wore, just those piss-stained underpants. His flesh stank of body odor and there were patches of crusted filth beneath the folds of his blubber. I got to see almost every little detail of him because we were intimately close when he was hurting me.

The box cutter was the worst part. He cut little pieces off of me, nothing important, but they left little holes all over me that made me feel broken and wrong. The tip of a pinky finger, a square from my heel, a sliver of my foreskin...so many little pieces. He put them all in a Mason jar and took them away afterwards

I never saw his face. He always wore a welder's mask when he came into the room. He never spoke to me; his only

12

communication came in the form of grunts and physical violence. Sometimes I caught a whiff of his breath from beneath the mask; it smelled sickly sweet, like candy-coated cancer. It became clear to me early on that he saw me as an object, not as a person.

I knew it was over when he brought in the propane torch. I was already terribly weak by then and I knew I wouldn't survive the blue horror of that flame. He'd already burnt me with lit cigarettes many times, but this was much worse.

At least the hopelessness would end.

He'd used me up and now what little remained of my life would be thrown away.

I blacked out when the flame of the torch kissed my neck.

I mistook the blackness for death.

***

I open my eyes to the world one last time. I am ruined; I know that the second cognitive thought returns to me. Pain assaults every single fiber of my being. My body hurts so much that I want to scream, but my tongue lies flat and dry in my mouth and it doesn't seem to work properly anymore. I'm like a cracked jar and all my vital fluids are dripping slowly out of me. He cooked parts of me and my skin hardened into little blackened strips, crispy and charred. Even the warm night air is excruciating as it blows against my burnt flesh.

My captor is carrying me like a doll he doesn't want anymore, a doll he's going to put into the trash. My eyes feel like they're smeared in Vaseline and the world is blurry and unreal. Every step the man takes sends bolts of agony sizzling through my head. He sucks greedily on a lollipop, a few specks of greenish spit oozing from the corner of his mouth to drip down into my hair.

He rounds a corner and stops in a narrow alleyway. He drops me on my side and I hit the ground hard, a shard of broken rib puncturing deeper into the inner parts of me that struggle to keep me alive. I try to roll onto my side but all I can manage is an inch or two. I see the huge blurry form of my captor prying at a manhole cover with a crowbar. He puts his back into it, working hard to get the heavy plate lifted and pushed off to the side.

A foul stench drifts up from the sewer below. I feel thick sausage fingers digging into my hair, pulling a few chunks out as he gets a good, solid grip. He lifts my entire body up like I weigh nothing at all. He offers me no words, no goodbye.

He's had his fun and now his fun is done.

He drops me through the opening and I fall far before crashing down against a set of filth-encrusted pipes. I land awkwardly on my side and a gusher of fresh blood sprays out of my left nostril. My face lies to the side and I can see one of my own hands floating in a little stream of human excrement. I try to move the fingers but I'm unable to do so, all I can manage is a weak twitch.

He's already sliding the manhole cover back into place somewhere above me, the light from the streetlamps being replaced by total darkness. I'm alone now, alone with the smell of the sewer and the hollow drip of fetid waste.

I am dying.

There's no doubting that. I feel the world slipping away; I feel my pain slowly but surely overcoming my survival instinct. I don't want to die here in a little river of piss and shit with no one to hold my hand and tell me it'll be alright. I don't want to die alone in the darkness. My mother will never know what happened to me. She's a single parent and she has tried so hard over the years.

I guess I'll never see her again.

The thought of my mother brings the tears. My tear ducts are ruined just like the rest of me so I barely manage a few salty droplets. I picture my life like a little light inside of me and I know that light is dimming now. No more school. No more catching toads. No more anything.

I take in a few final gasps of tainted oxygen and I wait to die.

3

Jack

The pitch blackness is settling in. I'm happy to give in and just let my eyes close. I reopen them just slightly though because I get the distinct feeling that I'm not alone down here anymore. I guess I must be hallucinating as death creeps closer. There's a presence approaching me, I feel it hovering above my prone body like a cloud of buzzing bees. I wish it would go away. I just want to sleep...

My vision is still so dark and blurry but the presence looks like a little cloud made of black and red particles. It floats and shifts above me, constantly changing shape. At one point it even looks like inky black eyes appear in the cloud, the eyes of some giant rat, but then they're gone again. Even in my ruined state I can feel the temperature of the little cloud. It's hellishly hot. Sweat beads across my brow as it hovers closer to me.

"Wakey, wakey..."

Did this intangible cloud just speak to me? The voice is hot and bubbly, a whisper caught in the embers of a furnace.

"You'll be dead in less than a few minutes. I'd suggest you hear me out."

I barely reply, trying desperately to turn my head away from this strange vision. My voice is choked and gurgled, clotted up with my own life's blood as it flows away from me.

"Lemme die."

"I totally could. That's kind of taking the pussy way out though, don't you think? This big stinky motherfucker abducts you, tortures you, and now leaves you to die in a pool of other people's shit. If that was me? I'd be a LITTLE bit pissed off..."

I have no idea who or what this is, but it's right. There's an undercurrent of anger slithering beneath all the pain my dying body is being tormented with. I hate this man for what he's done to me. I hate him for ruining me like this.

"Who are you?"

I let the question leave my bloody lips and hang there in the polluted air.

"Well…I'm gonna be honest with you, kid. I'm not God, I'm no angel, and I sure as shit ain't your dearly departed grandmother. I'm a demon. A minor demon, very low on Hell's totem pole, but I've still got a few tricks up my sleeves that could help you gain a little vengeance, if you want it. I was just floating around the Earthly plane and doing a little sightseeing…and being attracted as I am to violent moments, I couldn't help but notice your predicament."

I'm lying in a shallow stream of sewage and having a conversation with a demon.

Life sure is funny sometimes. And what little life remains to me is quickly running out…

"Let's get introductions outta the way! The name's Verminort. I'm from the thirteenth circle of Hell, I have dominion over rodents, and I enjoy long walks on the beach while looking out at a beautiful boiling ocean filled with mangled body parts. And you are?"

"You sound peachy."

A coughing fit tears through my chest. It feels very wet in there, my lungs drowning in my own blood.

"I'm Jack. Soon to be dead Jack. I'd shake your hand but I can't move my arms right now and you don't seem to have hands anyway…"

Hot laughter flows from the cloud, hitting me in the face like a blast of chili-flavored breath.

"Well I like your spunk, Soon to be dead Jack. Here's the thing. You don't necessarily have to die. Being a lesser demon, I'm pretty limited when it comes to badass powers and all that. Those are reserved for the dukes and kings of Hell. I am capable of possession though. If I were to possess you, all your wounds would heal. My essence alone would fix you right up."

Tempting. The cloud has moved closer to me, seeming to sense that my hearing is fading right along with the rest of me.

"What do I get outta this? I'm sure you're asking yourself that. I get to share your body with you for a little while and help you carry out a few atrocities on the vile man that left you in this sorry state. I get the thrill of having flesh and the thrill of using it. He's killed before, Jack. He'll do it again too. You're just

one victim on a pretty long list. I'm offering you a chance to pay him back...and stop him for good."

"Share my body? How's that work?"

"Think of it this way...we'll be like roommates! Your soul and my dark little essence renting the house that is your body. We make a simple pact. You invite me into you...and I help you put an end to the man that ruined you. The inviting part is important. More powerful demons, the big bads...they can just smash down the doors leading into people and possess them easily. You gotta open the door for me, Jack. You gotta let me in."

It's a tough choice. Die and let the monster that did this to me continue his reign of terror...or let this chatty demon into my body for just one chance at stopping the monster from killing again. I'm trying to mull it over while also trying to breathe. My throat seems to be far too moist.

"You're bleeding out, Jack. Choking on your own juices. I'm pretty much your last hope right now. As much as I enjoy the company of floating turds and dying boys, I can't really hang around forever. You gotta decide. Pact or no pact? Deal or no deal?"

I don't want to die in a place like this.

I want to see my mother again, I want to grow up, and I want to have a fighting chance at living my life. Most of all? I want my revenge. I shudder at the thought of letting a demon into my body, but at this point, I don't have many options on the table. It's this or death. It's gamble or die.

I let a weak, hollow sigh escape my lips.

"Deal."

The cloud is already changing shape all around me, becoming like swirling tendrils with pointed ends.

"Come on in."

The tendrils dart forward with deceptive speed and I feel the floating particles being pushed up through my nostrils and into my open mouth. I've opened the door. I've invited him in. Verminort blazes into his new home...and the old me dies.

4

Jack

The demon feels like acid pouring into my veins, eroding everything and remaking me from the inside out. The sensation is hideously alien, but there is little pain involved. If anything I feel the anguish slowly departing, my failing form starting to feel healthy and whole again. I'm convulsing, my limbs clawing and flapping through the little streams of foulness all around me.

I immediately become aware of the *other* inside of me, a piece of antimatter lodged into my brain. The whirling black and red cloud that is Verminort slithers through my mind, seeming to acquaint himself with his new surroundings. My flesh is stitching itself together. The little pieces that were taken from me are growing fresh again. My blood seeps back into me and floods anew into my heart, strengthening the dying organ. The entire process makes me feel itchy.

My back arches up violently and sewer water flies from my clothes. My spine seems to contort and retract, realigning itself. I feel a surge of low, hot power traveling through my limbs. My body temperature rises dramatically. Little puffs of steam exit through my nostrils. I become dimly aware of sewer rats gathering on the dripping pipes above, watching this event unfold with something like rodent rapture.

A roar escapes my lips and echoes through the dank underground corridors. It's bestial, full of hedonistic excitement. I catch sight of my eyes in a little pool of fetid waste. Once blue, now obsidian black. The convulsions are departing now, replaced by a pleasant warmness, pins and needles dancing across my skin.

I don't feel invaded. I don't feel any loss of control. I feel *merged*. It's like having a shadow inside of you, matching every move you make, increasing your strength, your speed, your ability to endure. I can feel him in there though. I can feel Verminort exploring and getting comfortable.

I'm able to sit up and drag my back up against the tunnel wall. Desperation is reserved for the dying. I'm not dying now. Truthfully I've never felt more alive.

I look down at the sections of my body that my captor ruined. They've been restored, crisscrossed with the faintest shade of white scar tissue.

I am remade.

I am reborn.

I am saved.

Not just Jack.

Not just Verminort.

A conglomeration of the two, a young soul and a dark essence melded together in the confines of this boymeat.

Now...we are *one*.

***

"Helluva ride, huh?"

The voice is a cheerful rhythm in my head. The demon sounds incredibly pleased, much like a junkie after getting a really good fix. I test my right hand, curling the fingers and balling it up into a fist. There's a little mark on the tip of my pinky finger where the skin and fingernail regenerated. That's pretty cool.

"So, uh...what happens now?"

"Well, we demons are bound to any deal we make. If memory serves our deal consists of tracking down the sadistic porker that did this to you and giving him a little taste of Hell. Sound about right to you?"

"Sounds perfect."

"So glad we agree, roomie! Couple ground rules though. We're bound by this frail twelve year old meat-vehicle. As I told you, I don't have a shitload of mystical powers like the high society demons do. I'm pretty much lower middle class. That means we have to be careful. This flesh can be hurt. It can be maimed. This body we share can even be killed. If we lose parts now, we don't regenerate. That was a one-time thing."

"That complicates matters a bit."

"Only a little! It just means we can't bum rush this guy on some half-assed kamikaze mission and try to take him down in

19

a fair fight. He's big, he's bad...and he's fully capable of squashing this body all over again. We have to strategize. We need to plan. That's the key to ridding Greyfield of Edgar."

"You know his name?"

I rub a hand against my arm, almost like I'm feeling that box cutter slicing into my skin all over again.

"He never told me his name. Never spoke to me at all. He was just faceless, nasty...nothing but hurt on two legs."

"Yeah. Big donkey-brained son of a bitch isn't the most eloquent talker. You didn't miss out on much, so don't feel bad."

I surprise myself by laughing. It feels good to laugh after coming within inches of dying in a dark sewer tunnel.

"As I was saying, you're not gonna get an instant kill even with me inside of you. I can't strike him down with a ball of hellfire or suddenly grow horns and gore him or anything like that. We're bound by this flesh and we gotta make that work. Luckily for you...I'm resourceful. I'm crafty. I'm also an expert when it comes to inflicting the prettiest pain your sweet little eyes ever did see!"

"That'll come in handy..."

"Our darling Edgar—Sweets to his nonexistent friends—is a creature of habit. He's sloppy in his personal life but careful when it comes to his little hobby of butchering boys and girls. I know his routine. I know how to track him. It's just about picking the most opportune moment to strike."

It all sounds good. A few nagging doubts still float through my mind though. I can't tell if Verminort can read my thoughts or not, but for the moment it seems like they're cut off from him. I certainly can't pick up on his thoughts.

"So after he's dead and the deal is done, what happens to us?"

"I depart. This little body is yours and yours alone once again, and you can do whatever you please with it up until the day you die. The deal is I help you kill Edgar. I never go back on a deal. I'm literally incapable of doing that."

"Okay. Sounds fair."

"Yup. But in the meantime, I'm looking to enjoy this flesh a little bit. Feels DAMN good to be all up in this carnal meat. It's *actually my first time possessing someone. I guess that makes me kind of a demonic virgin..."*

"Uhhh...you didn't mention that before?"

"Don't even worry about it! I got this. We're a team, Jack. How bout we fuel up, roomie? I'm starving. We have a big day ahead of us tomorrow, after all."

Verminort exerts control over the body and I feel my left hand lift up, the fingers snapping a few times. A plump sewer rat suddenly climbs down from some piping above and starts to scurry across the floor towards us.

"Told you I have a few tricks up my infernal sleeve."

"You're not serious. We're gonna eat...that?"

"Don't knock it until you've tried it, Jack! These little buggers are full of nutrients and shit."

One of our hands snakes forward and takes hold of the rat, the hairy little critter climbing happily into our palm. The fingers close and there's a terrible crunch sound followed by a dying squeak.

I guess dinner is served.

5

Jack 2.0

There's a fire pit in my backyard at home and I like to light it some evenings after school and just sit there in front of it, watching the flames crackling and the embers floating up into the air. Lucky for me I always keep an old pack of matches in my pocket for that purpose. I let Verminort take control of the skinning and preparing of the rodent. He does it with hideous precision, the scummy little pelt getting peeled back like a false face, showing only glistening meat beneath.

I focus on getting the fire going, using bits and pieces of discarded toilet tissue and rotten newspaper that made it down here through the drainage grates. The tinder catches quickly and we have a warm little campfire blazing in one of the only dry corners to be found in the filthy sewer tunnel.

Once the plump carcass of the rat is skewered on the makeshift spit (made out of a broken section of corroded pipe) I can't help but feel deepening hunger pangs in my gut. The smell of cooking meat drives me wild and surprises me too. I never thought I'd be craving roasted rat but after the personal Hell I've been through...this little meal stinks of pure heaven.

During my incarceration Edgar kept me alive on saltine crackers and lukewarm boiled water, so I'm sure that plays into the desperate longing in my belly. After the rat has been sufficiently toasted I reach out and tear a strip of flesh from the charred meat, proceeding to gobble it down greedily. It's divine, full of gamey flavor that burns my tongue just slightly and slides down my throat like a pleasant lump.

"Can I just state for the record...human taste buds are fuckin' awesome. Oh my Lucifer, can it get any better than this?"

"It tastes kind of like deer meat. My uncle is a hunter and he used to bring me and my mom home deer steaks all the time when I was little."

"You're still little, Jack. We'll have to work around that when it comes time to brutalize a fat man. Don't sweat it, though. I'm full of bright ideas."

My fingers are sticky with the blood and grease of the rat, the whole little body held between my hands now as I chomp into it. I try to talk and chew at the same time.

"So, um…what's Hell like?"

I'm not big on conversation, especially when it comes to making small talk with a demon.

It's the best effort I can put forth.

"Honestly? Hell sucks, roomie. I grew up in the thirteenth circle, super rough neighborhood. Basically a demonic ghetto, the lowest of the low. Makes this fancy ass sewer look like a Hollywood mansion. My father kicked me into a pit of meat-maggots the moment after I was born, so I guess it's safe to say I have some abandonment issues."

I suck at the hip bones of the rat, slurping in the sizzling juices of the little critter and getting as much sustenance into me as I can.

"You humans don't realize how good you have it. You guys and girls can be whatever you want when you grow up. A fireman, a police officer, a fuckin' astronaut! We demons have only one career option. Torturer. Gotta deal with lousy shithead souls all day and night—the worst of the worst—and it gets so ridiculously boring. They scream, they cry, they poop on themselves…yeah; even souls can poop on themselves if you torture them bad enough. No raises, no career advancement…I don't even have health insurance down there."

"That seems…awful. So is it like it is in the movies? All fiery and stuff?"

"Nah. Not anymore. Just like the Earthly plane, Hell is always evolving. That fire and brimstone crap went out in the 1920s. The only demons down there that still have hooves and goat horns are certified granddaddies about to kick the piss-filled bucket. These days…Hell is modern. We're all about very personal torments. We take the most important aspects of your lives, your most cherished memories, and we corrupt them and twist them until they drive you batshit crazy. Once you've seen those you love the most turned into defiled revenants that exist only to feed into your suffering…you're gonna break pretty quickly."

A little shiver travels through me as Verminort describes that particular style of torment. I can't even imagine some vile thing masquerading as my mother for the sole purpose of breaking my spirit.

I wipe my grubby hands along the front of my shirt. The rat grease mixes in with the blood and sewer water that already saturates the material. I'm desperately in need of a shower, but something tells me that won't be happening anytime soon.

"When can I go home?"

"Not a good idea, roomie. Not yet. Showing up on momma's doorstep while infused with a demonic presence isn't really the Hallmark card homecoming anyone is looking for. After we deal with Edgar and after I've returned your body to you, then you can go home. Until that point, this Fortress of Sewer Solitude will be our temporary resting place."

I'm a little disappointed but I figured that would be the case. The idea of returning to my mother's house with Verminort inside of me doesn't seem like the right path to take right now.

Edgar comes first.

"Now that mister rat is in all gobbled up, I think it's time for this body to rest a little. We have to conserve as much strength as we can from now on. Gotta be ready, Jack. Tomorrow we do a little recon. Know thy enemy, young grasshopper."

I'm already crawling closer to the fire and curling up, my mind and body exhausted after everything that's happened.

"I won't argue with that."

The warmth of the little fire feels good against my skin. The meat feels good in my belly. The idea of what I'm going to do to Edgar when we finally catch up to him feels best of all.

I fall deeply asleep with a small smile creeping across my mouth.

6

Jack 2.0

I don't know how long I've slept. A few rays of midday sun shine through one of the drainage grates farther down the tunnel and the glint of light catches me directly in the eyes. The fire burned down at some point overnight, leaving only a little pile of faintly smoking ash. It's chilly and dank down here in the sewer without the fire, but I barely even notice it. There seems to be constant warmth inside of me now, swirling and electric...one of the perks of being possessed by a demon, I suppose.

"Good afternoon, sleeping beauty. Fancy a bit of orange juice?"

I rise up, stretching and yawning. I run a hand through my grimy hair and shake some of the previous night away.

"I'd love some."

"I was just fuckin' with ya. This is a sewer, kid. You lemme know if you spot an orange tree down here."

"Rude."

I'm already climbing up to my feet and brushing some of the less than desirable crud from my clothes. I even put on a brave face and sniff at my armpit. I smell like shit. I guess that's a byproduct of sleeping in a place built to contain shit.

"I'll tell you what I do have, though. I've got a little stroll planned for us today. The sewer tunnels beneath Greyfield are very old and very intricate. This place is practically a labyrinth. A labyrinth our proverbial Minotaur named Edgar knows very well. Thankfully for us he only ventures down here when he's got a body to dump..."

I'm already walking down the dim corridor. I feel Verminort in my head like a demonic GPS system, guiding me around sharp corners and leading me deeper into the maze of the sewer system. We make our way to a little ramp composed of a steel mesh walkway, stagnant greenish water lying undisturbed beneath our feet.

"What exactly are we looking for?"

"A very particular window. A window where we can see him but he can't see us. It's all about stealth, roomie. Imagine yourself as a 12 year old ninja going after the biggest, ugliest toad you ever did see. You know a thing or two about that, don't ya?"

"Yeah. But this isn't a toad I want to keep and care for."

I feel that hot, impotent hate coursing through my veins again. The same hate I felt when I was chained to that busted radiator. It makes a little vein pulse in my temple with each step I take. It seems to travel out from me in waves, and I'm sure it helped Verminort to find me in the first place.

"This is one I want to squash."

"That's the spirit. Hate is hip, Jackie boy. Let that hate grow inside of you. Picture it like a twisted tree that you're watering with acid and feeding with severed limbs. Let it grow big and tall, and let it cast a long shadow. When the time comes, we're gonna use every bit of it."

We walk for what seems like a long time. The corridors wind deeper and deeper through the hidden bowels of Greyfield. Sometimes the tunnels narrow to the point where I have to creep through them sideways and other times I have to crouch down and practically crawl through overflow pipes.

After we've been walking along in silence for awhile we round a bend and enter into a fairly large circular room. This section of the sewer appears much older than the rest, the walls corroded and eaten away completely in certain partitions. Algae growth is mucked across the lower walls and I catch sight of a slick black water snake gliding away from us as we enter. The snake came out of the pant's leg of a little pair of brown trousers, waterlogged and forgotten.

There's an entire pile of children's clothing down here. Some of the items float through the fetid water and a great soaked bundle remains leaning up against a far wall. Tiny dresses, t-shirts depicting popular cartoon characters, even little shoes can be found among the pile.

I'm standing up to my ankles in water and I notice something drifting across the murky surface towards me. I kneel down to pick it up. It's a hair band decorated in bright pink butterflies, the kind a little girl would wear. I stare down at this, my hand tightening across the torn material.

That hatred is rising up within me all over again. I'm surrounded by lost innocence. Memories of those that fell far too early in life, the only remnants left of them blotted away in this dark and lonely place. Little lives extinguished by the inhuman desires of a selfish *fuck* that tore me away from everything I knew. A lump grows in my throat and I can practically taste the sorrow. These children deserved better than this. They deserved to grow up and grow old. They deserved a *chance*.

"He's been doing this for a long time, Jack. Most of these kids were much younger than you."

I won't cry for them. Anyone can cry for them and do nothing about it.

I'll avenge them instead.

"He'll never stop. I know his type. They destroy and they defile and they never, ever stop. He won't stop...unless we stop him."

I let the little hair band fall from my hand back into the water. It floats along a faint current before disappearing into another channel.

"We're close now. Let's keep going."

We leave the chamber of lost children and continue down another corridor, this one lined along the upper portion with many holes opening up on the streets outside, slivers of sunlight passing inward from the sewer drains.

The corridor ends at a large elbow pipe leading up to yet another sewer drain. I climb up, Verminort momentarily assuming control when my hand slides on a slippery section of pipe. Finally we gain our balance and I'm able to gaze out through the sewer drain, my eyes squinted against the sunlight.

I'm looking at a familiar place. It's the auto body shop out on Cherry Street. I've passed by that place tons of times. It's on the school bus route I take each morning and evening. As I watch a tow truck cruises into view in front of the shop and approaches one of the open garage doors.

It reads "Malencourt Automotive Services" on the driver's side door with a smiling tire painted beneath.

The door opens with a creak and the entire truck shifts as the massive driver exits and stands there with the sun glinting down on his ruddy features. A dirty hat is pulled down low across his face; draping most of it in shadow...but his mouth is visible. The lips are thick and wormy, almost oddly feminine. There's a lollipop stick jutting out from them.

My captor. My torturer.

My enemy.

"Seems we're right on time."

***

"This place? I've passed by it so many times..."

I can't help but shake my head. I watch as the vile giant lumbers off into his garage, pausing only to make sure that the automatic garage door closes behind him. It comes as no surprise to me that he wants his privacy.

"The bastard has been here all along."

"Hiding in plain sight, you might say. No one suspects him. He runs his modest local business, pays his taxes, and tips his hat to everyone who greets him. Just big ol' harmless Edgar...loves his sweets and wouldn't hurt a fly. That's his public image, Jack. His private image is entirely different. You've experienced the darkness this man keeps hidden away inside of himself..."

I certainly have. Even though I'm healed, those little sections of my body still covered with fresh scar tissue seem to burn and sting all over again. There's nothing comparable to that...feeling violated and forever ruined. It scars the psyche just as much as the flesh.

"This is a little slice of Hell on the Earthly plane, Jack. Mark it well with your eyes. A flimsy veil stretched across a nexus of human evil. The veil has held for a long time, and it will hold a bit longer...unless we rip it away and expose all of Edgar's little secrets."

"I thought we'd get a little more....personal with him. Brutally personal."

"Oh we will, roomie, don't misunderstand. There is exquisite brutality in Edgar Malencourt's near future, but first we weaken

his resolve. He feels safe and faceless in his cradle of anonymity. Even a lion will grow fat and lazy if he remains unchallenged for a long period of time. First...we challenge the lion. We rattle him and tease him. We encourage him to slip, to fall off his game just a little."

"How do we do that?"

"Easy. We let him know that we know."

Realization dawns on me like the pleasant light of a new sunrise, and it inspires a dry little smile to take shape across my lips.

"We'll need a bit of paper and something to write with. Edgar doesn't know it yet, but he'll be receiving a special note from us tonight."

"I'm game for that, but how will we get a note to him?"

"We'll do it just like the postal service does it. We'll stick it right into his grimy little mailbox."

We're already sliding down off the pipe and heading back down the sewer corridor in the direction we came from. I feel Verminort leading me again, showing me the right path.

"Next stop...House Malencourt."

7

Edgar

Garage always got a powerful stink to it. Smells like grease and metal and oil. Always like getting me a big whiff of it when I walk in. This old place been in my family for generations, my daddy ran it before he kicked the bucket and my grandpappy before him. Daddy smoked too many cigars and burnt his lungs up until they was all black. They did an autopsy on him and pulled them lungs outta his chest like two pieces of meat that spoiled and went bad.

I ain't never touched no cigarette and I never will. Smoking the worst kinda habit a man can have. It eat up all the money in your pocket and leave nothing but ash to show for it. I just like my candy, my lollipops in particular. I like to suck them pops' til the stick just as clean as can be. That's my addiction, but it ain't nothing all that bad. I got me a gut but that just run in the family too, genetics and all that. All the Malencourts were big men, we just built that way.

I'm the last man in the Malencourt bloodline now. It's up to me to keep the legacy alive now that my daddy and all my uncles are just dead and in the dirt. I didn't do no good in school and I was always a bit simple, but I got me a real talent for fixing cars. I can look at an engine and put my ear to it and know just what's wrong. It might be knocking or chugging or smoking, but don't matter none, I can get to the bottom of it real quick. I'm mighty good at my job and I ain't got no trouble keeping the family business going.

I like fixing stuff...but it ain't my passion.

That's just a job. Everybody got to have a job and act normal otherwise you stick out in the world like a sore thumb. I learned when I was still just a young buck that blending in is better than sticking out. That's why I was always careful whenever I hurt the little animals I'd find. I'd clean up real good afterwards and I'd make sure nobody saw nothin'.

I was just a little kid then and I was still learning bout the stuff I liked. It's wonderful when you find something you like though, it feels special and it was like I knew what I'd been put on this earth to do. Sometimes I'd catch me a little chipmunk and twist the neck around til I heard a brittle crack. The eyes would bug out and the tongue would flop out too and I really liked that a lot. I always liked springtime because you could find bird nests all over the place. My favorite thing was taking down the nest with them little naked baby birds chirping at me, and then I would bring my boot down on them real slow and grind them into mush.

My best memory was finding me a dog got ran over by a semi truck on the highway one afternoon. His legs were all twisted up and he was panting something fierce, but he was still very much alive. I think he was a Labrador but it was hard to tell because his fur was all matted up with blood. I made sure there weren't any nosy people around and I dragged that dog into the woods.

I took my time with it and got him to a nice little clearing. I wanted it to be a quiet and secret place so that I could savor things. I had me a little pocket knife that my daddy gave me for my birthday one year and I took it out and stabbed it into the dog a few times. I did it real slow and only put the blade in a few inches each time. I started on his broken legs and then moved up his body to his chest and neck. He'd make this little whimper sound in his throat and he was hurting so much, I could see the hurt in them big ol' brown eyes he had.

There ain't no mistaking the look of hurt. It's dark and deep and there's no hope to be found in it. Always reminded me of looking down into a well that just keeps on descending and never really ends. I love staring down into the hurt. It's a fascinating thing and I could do that forever and be real happy.

I knew I'd discovered my calling after I stabbed that dog about fifty seven times.

He finally died after I stabbed him the fifty eighth time.

See, it ain't about death for me. I don't much care about killing things, that don't get me off or give me any kind of special feeling. Death is just the inevitable part of hurting a living thing. It's just a secondary thing that can't be avoided one way or the other. It's the *hurt* that interests me. I got an addiction to seeing the pain on a face that's going through

31

some serious suffering. I never been much for reading books or any of that shit, but one time I heard me a word in a movie and I looked it up in the dictionary afterwards. That word was sadist. It means "someone who obtains pleasure from inflicting pain on others".

There ain't never been a better description of me. That's exactly what it is, right there in that fancy sounding word. It's everything that I am. It's what I was born to be. It's all I want and there ain't nothin' better in life, not even the sweetest lollipop or humping my sister til I squirt up inside her. There ain't a damn thing that compares to inflicting that *hurt* and seeing what it does to someone up close.

I gotta be careful now, though. The cops round Greyfield been sniffing around and trying to find out what's going on. They ain't got no idea I'm the one they looking for. I've been lucky and I'm real good bout cleaning up after myself.

I gotta get my *hurt* but I gotta be smart about it. I've come too far now to get locked up in the pen. That boy playing near the frog pond gave me some good hurt but he didn't last long enough. He withered up too quick and I had to dump him down the shit-chute.

I gotta get me another one soon.

I got the perfect one picked out, too.

She gonna suffer so good, and I just know she'll look purdy doing it.

8

Edgar

She's such a precious little nubbin of a child. She can't be no older than six or seven, I'd warrant. I've got the tow truck parked beneath some oaks, the shade of them feeling good on this hot summer day. I'm still sweating mighty fierce though. Big ol' fella like me can't help but sweat when it's hot and he sees somethin purdy.

I ain't sure what her name is. I heard her momma call out the front door to her once when she was playing in the yard, somethin like Tiffany or Tanya maybe. Ain't rightly sure. Don't matter none anyhow, I'll get her name later. She's the perfect one. She'll hurt beautifully; I'm assured of that the moment I see her skipping off the big yellow school bus.

She got the deepest red hair like flames on her head and the cutest little freckles across the apples of her cheeks. She's wearing a baby blue top and baby blue pants. She's just a little baby all covered in blue. Her little backpack is hot pink and the face of a teddy bear decorates it. She's got a tiny smile on her face now, enjoying the fresh freedom of the day after getting off the school bus. I watch the bus pull away. I watch *her* most of all.

Most people would probably mistake me for a kiddie diddler or somethin. That ain't even close to the truth. I hate them nasty old fuckers that touch on kids like that. I don't get no sexy feelings from looking at them or touching them. For me it's all about the hurt. Children are innocent; children are untainted by the world. Children are honest and humble about everything that happens to them, nothing held back.

Children feel the hurt best of all.

I tap and drum my fingers on the steering wheel, just appreciating the target in the distance. Now ain't the time to take her. This ain't the right place and it ain't the moment. I've always had me a strong intuition about the right moment.

It's gotta be perfect. The wind gotta be blowing just the right way and you gotta feel like you're untouchable in the act.

I've lasted this long because I'm careful. Many watchful eyes in Greyfield do nothing but see, but all the eyes in Greyfield just don't see me. I lick my lollipop and I relish the momentary breeze that floats in through my rolled down window. Little Red don't notice me way down here parked in the shade. She's too busy ruffling the head of the little white terrier that runs across the yard to greet her. He's an old, feeble dog, I can tell that just by looking at him. I'd snap him up easy, like many brittle twigs.

It won't be today...but it's gonna be soon.

Little Red gonna feel some hurt.

I fire up the tow truck's engine and I ease on out of my parking spot, proceeding to roll on down the road toward the home place. An old man who lives at the house next to my victim's house waves at me while watering his rose bushes.

I raise up a hand and wave right back.

Most people know me pretty well in town. I'm well liked and got the respect of my neighbors.

They never see me coming.

9

Edgar

It's late in the day when I pull up to the old home place. A twisty dirt road leads up a hill and there at the top sits the crumbling mansion of the Malencourts. She ain't no beauty. She might have been once, but the wear and tear of decades had stripped her of anything that could be thought of as easy on the eyes. I ain't gotten around to giving her a new coat of paint, being so busy all the time with my little hobbies. She's all warped brown wood and little tendrils of white paint that Mother Nature has ripped and clawed at with her windy fingernails.

Her angles are sharp and her windows are murky. She looms on that hill and everything below her withers beneath her gaze. She's an ugly old bitch of a house but there's something foreboding about her. She's got this dreadful look...and I've always liked that. The house been in the family as long as I can remember. She was built in the early 1800s and she used to be a plantation house. My grandpappy used to tell me that you can still find some slave bones down in the dirt of the basement if you dig down far enough. There are rusty old shackles up in the attic too, decorated in cobwebs. They've been there since the old days.

I pull the tow truck into the familiar parking spot beside the front door and I kill the engine. The truck bounces when I exit and shift my weight to the ground. Life as a big-boned man sure does present challenges.

I pull the key ring from my belt and open up the front door. It smells pretty scuzzy and the lighting in the foyer is low. I like the scuzzy smell, it's familiar. I like the low lighting too. I ain't never trusted a man or woman who can sit under them bright ass fluorescents and smile at you like they ain't bothered. There's something unnatural about that. Life ain't no damn fun if there ain't shadows to play in.

I got many padlocks and deadbolts on the front door from the inside. I make sure to lock them all before getting comfortable. I head towards the kitchen and the special little place beyond the kitchen. It's almost always my first stop when I get back to the house. It soothes me after a long, hard day. I don't put no damn stock into yoga and meditation and all that new age shit, but there is something powerful in my little space. Makes me feel good when I'm in there. Makes me feel strong.

I pass by the long kitchen table, a few plates still sitting on it with uneaten food. A wriggling mass of maggots are in the process of being born in a little hollow of ancient meatloaf on a dirty blue plate. Guess I'll have to throw that out soon. Damn shame...that was a good meatloaf.

The door to the pantry (my special space) connects directly with the kitchen. It's pretty narrow and looks like the entrance to a closet or something. I open her up and step on in, closing the door behind me. It's dark until I reach up and pull a cord to illuminate my surroundings. A single bare bulb hangs down from the ceiling, swinging from side to side to cast flickering illumination across the impressive collection I got in here.

There's a stool in the middle of the pantry. It squat and sturdy and it's always supported my weight. I hunker down on it now, taking a moment to sweep my eyes around the multiple rows of shelves on the walls. I built those shelves myself and I'm proud of how they look. I'm even prouder of the many, many jars that are featured on the shelves, the source of this room's power.

My *sweet treats*...

10

Edgar

The swinging glow from the bulb flashes off the glass of so many purdy jars. They're all labeled with names. I'm real good about organizing em' like that. There's little Billy up on the top shelf, and Cindy down below. Jake and Stu were twins so I put their jars together on the third shelf down. I've got all my children up there. A collection of hurt.

Each jar holds a few little pieces of the ones I've lead into boundless suffering. Sometimes it's an ear. Sometimes a little pinky finger or a big toe. Sometimes it's a little piece of their genitals or a chunk of hair ripped clean outta the scalp. So many tiny pieces of flesh, so many bits and scraps of the little person that felt the hurt. It's all that remains of them. Their bodies are long gone, some to the sewer, others to the dirt in the forest, some to the furnace in the basement.

All that is left is right here. Just the *sweet treats* floating in greenish formaldehyde. The colors kinda wash over the walls and over my face too, making it seem like I'm floating in a weird green ocean and seeing all these little body parts floating by me. An eyeball with trailing nerve tissue from four shelves up, a severed tongue from the bottom shelf. All the parts drift on by me and I can name them all. Ain't got the best memory so that's why I put those labels on em'.

I'm feeling good now. So damn calm. My eyelids start to feel heavy and I just let the vibes wash over me. Somewhere on the second story of the house I hear a powerful squealing and someone knocking furniture against the floor. That can wait, though.

I'm fixing to savor my time here for as long as I can.

***

I keep her up in a little bedroom with the windows blacked out from the inside, taped over with trash bags. She ain't seen the sunshine since we were little kids playing tag out in the yard.

All I permit in the room is a single candle flame when I'm in here with her. It's easier for me to get hard when I don't gotta look at her. I don't wanna see the degradation of her form, the scum that covers her body and the broken pleas that swirl in her foolish mind. I don't wanna see her face and I don't wanna look into her eyes.

She's just meat to be pounded. Flesh to be fucked. A big ol' ball of nasty for me to slip my johnson into when I get that funny little feeling. I promised momma before she died that I'd take care of little Sue. Sue wasn't never meant to survive on her own out in this cold, hard world. She wouldn't last a day out there. They'd ship her off to one of those retard homes and she'd spend the rest of her life there eating government pudding and taking orders from strangers.

It's better that she be kept in the family like this. I ain't never looked down on her for having Down syndrome, ain't never made fun of her for it or nothin like that. She gets on my fuckin' nerves sometimes when she squeals and whines but sticking a dirty sock in her mouth takes care of that right quick.

It's my job to take care of my sister now and I've done the best I can. I feed her every day and night, sometimes pig slop and sometimes her favorite foods, like meatloaf and tater chips. She don't know the difference...just slurps it all down like a vacuum cleaner. I change her bedpan too; make sure to clean the piss and shit out of it real good before putting it back under her.

I'm a big-boned man...but my little sister makes me look small. She's a whale of a girl, weighing in at about six hundred pounds. She's totally bedridden and couldn't leave this room even if she wanted to, her ass alone wouldn't fit through the doorframe. I'd have to knock the damn wall down just to get her through. I guess she's what all them fancy doctors would call morbidly obese. That ain't never made me love her any less, though. She's a good girl with an empty head, that's all.

She's always followed me around everywhere since we were little kids. She used to be like a little puppy dog around me. I got real tired of that after momma died. I always worried Sue would blunder into the pantry and accidentally mess with my sweet treats. Plus she's a damn handful to keep up with...and I ain't got time to baby-sit her all day and night. A man like me would go damn near insane without his hobbies.

I guess that's why I decided to cut off her arms and legs and tie her to the bed.

I left her some pretty decent stumps, though. Cut her hands off at the forearms so she can still swing her elbows around when she wants somethin. Her legs I severed at the shins...and I'll tell you what, there ain't nothin harder in life than trying to saw through a shin bone. Talk about a god damn workout! The wounds have healed up pretty good over the years. I stuffed some antibiotics and such into her meatloaf to make sure infection wouldn't set in. It was for her own good. Ain't safe for a retard to be running around the house by herself all day when I'm working and doing my business.

I've been real good to Sue. Best big brother a gal could ask for. That's why I think it's alright to fuck her now and then. I'm entitled to a little pleasure due to how much I've sacrificed for my sister. There's a big ol' rope that I've got fastened around her belly meat and I just take hold of that and pump into her like a jackhammer til I squirt right on them folds of flab. I think she kinda likes it. Hard to tell. She makes that squeal sound all the time so kinda tough to get an idea of what she's thinking or feelin'.

She's squealing for me now. The bed is creaking against the floorboards and the only reason it don't collapse is because I reinforced it underneath with concrete blocks. She stinks to high heaven but that kinda makes me even hornier, she just got such a heavy aroma...like an aphrodisiac.

There's a little sliver of moonlight coming in from the window where a piece of the trash bag has come loose. I'll have to fix that later. It shines on fat, pimply skin and a puckered mouth full of broken teeth. I pull a bit of the blanket up to cover that ugly mug of hers. Don't need it ruining my fun.

The orgasm shakes through my body like an earthquake, my whole body jiggling on top of hers.

Makes me damn near howl at the moon.

11

Jack 2.0

The little metal door of the mailbox swings closed, the note safely deposited within alongside all the junk mail. Night has fallen and there's no possibility of anyone seeing us way down here, especially because the lane snakes so far away from the house on the hill. And what a terrible eyesore House Malencourt is, seeming both malevolent and tarnished all at the same time. It's hard to make out the features of the house by the starlight, but what I do see of it makes me feel dirty. It makes me want to bleach my entire soul.

"Feel it, don't ya? The undercurrent of evil that emanates from that house. I pick up on it like a very powerful radio station. Edgar might as well throw up a billboard in the front yard that says SICK SHIT HAPPENS HERE."

Verminort couldn't put it any better. Just being this close to the house unnerves me…and this is coming from a kid who's possessed by a demon.

"The people of Greyfield might be blind to it, but take it from me; Jack my boy…this place is a nest for darkened dreams. Twisted desires have grown here and they've been fed here. It's part of this town's history…just a hushed, hidden part."

"Where do we go now? Back to the sewer?"

"Nah. We'll spend a night under the stars enjoying the fresh air. Besides, our shared body is starting to smell like the shits Leviathan takes after he's binged on about a thousand tortured souls…"

"It's that bad?"

I can't help but sniff at my saturated t-shirt. It definitely is.

"We can't all smell like petunias, kiddo. That's life."

I've started down a cracked sidewalk, making sure to keep to the shadows and out of the glow cast by the streetlamps. It wouldn't be good for me to be spotted in this condition.

"Do you think maybe we should leave town until it's time to take Edgar down? We're really exposed out here…maybe we could hole up in Charles Town or Rust Valley for a few days."

Suddenly my feet stop dead center on the sidewalk. There's the slightest twinge in my head...and it takes me a moment to realize that it's Verminort twitching with fear. I didn't think demons could even fall victim to fear.

"We're not going anywhere near Rust Valley, Jack. That is the place where the dirt king sleeps, and woe onto those that hear the lullabies from beneath."

"Uhh...what are you talking about?"

"There are some things in this universe that are older and stranger even than the Pit, Jack. Ancient, forgotten things that even the grandest lords and dukes of Hell know to cower before. Rust Valley is home to one of these things. Something beyond time, beyond death, beyond everything..."

"What kind of things?"

My legs are my own again and I continue walking forward, Verminort guiding me towards a particularly tall sycamore tree across the street.

"Unknowable things. Things you're better off not thinking about."

I pause before the tree, looking up into many dark limbs that reach ever higher towards the stars in the sky.

"Besides, we wanna be close to our bulbous target. I think I've got a pretty good idea of how Malencourt is gonna react when he finds our little letter, but we gotta play this thing close to the chest. No room for errors."

That much I can definitely agree with. We can't risk this man continuing the reign of butchery he started in this town. If we don't stop this, I truly believe it'll never stop...

"Time for bed. Lemme show you how flexible this bod of ours is, roomie!"

Suddenly I feel my limbs contorting and twisting in unnatural angles and I'm LAUNCHED forward into the bark of the tree, my fingers and shoes digging up into the trunk. I begin climbing it at an incredibly disturbing pace, my joints cracking and creaking, my movements like that of a jumping spider.

Finally Verminort swings our body forward onto one of the highest limbs and we spin erratically before coming to rest on rough bark, a few leaves coming dislodged and drifting down to the street below. As I look down I'm momentarily amazed at how far we've come up the tree. Good thing I'm not afraid of heights.

"Impressed?"

"More like nauseous."

"It'll pass! Get comfy. We've got a perfect view of House Malencourt from here and the leaves will keep us camouflaged. I'll keep you from falling outta the tree if our body starts to slide…and I'll be sure to wake you up in the morning."

I surprise myself by stretching out across the thick sycamore limb. I take a few handfuls of leaves and make myself a rudimentary pillow. I'm actually pretty comfortable up here…

"So you've got an alarm clock function too, Verminort? You're way cooler than my cell phone."

"Go to sleep, wiseass."

I follow my demon's advice. My eyelids start to droop, the last sight I see a canopy of dark leaves above me, covering me in blankets of shadow. A few solitary bats circle overhead. I count the rotations they make before drifting away into peaceful blackness.

12

Jack 2.0

"Ding, ding, ding! Other annoying buzzing and beeping sounds, etc etc."

I groggily roll to the side, my hand reaching up to adjust my pillow a bit beneath my head. I can't seem to get it to fluff out all the way.

"You're a shitty alarm clock. Where's the snooze button?"

The words are slurred leaving my mouth, my mind already sinking back down into the familiarity of sleep. Suddenly I'm shook and rattled from the inside, my whole body seeming to vibrate. My eyes snap open and I remember that I'm extremely high up in a tree, my arms and legs draping over the sides of the limb and a little pool of drool collected on my makeshift pillow of leaves.

"The man of the hour has arrived. See for yourself."

The familiar sight of the gunmetal gray tow truck rolling down the dirt road is the first thing I notice when I crane my neck around to look beyond the limbs of the sycamore. I can just make out Edgar's meaty hands on the wheel and his grease-stained work shirt, but the glare from the sun on the windshield blots out the features of his face.

He reaches the end of the lane and leans out of the open driver's side window to unlatch his mailbox, proceeding to take the entire bundle of mail in hand before tossing it indifferently into the passenger seat. He doesn't seem to immediately notice the letter, no doubt obscured by junk mail and colorful advertisements.

"Damn. Looks like we're gonna have to tail him for awhile, roomie. We have to be sure that he sees the letter."

The tow truck is already turning down the road and heading east in the direction of downtown Greyfield. Many planted sycamores line the sidewalks leading in that direction, bordering the road like monoliths.

"Hold on tight...and enjoy the ride."

Before I even have a chance to ask what that means, Verminort is swinging our shared body from the limb of the tree and LEAPING through the air before we crash onto another tree several feet away. My fingers dig into the bark and gain purchase, then we push off with our feet and launch right into the next tree, flipping and twisting through the air like an extremely agile spider.

This pace continues as we pursue Malencourt's tow truck, the wind blasting against my face with each leap forward through the foliage.

13

Edgar

Such a beautiful day. I've always been a morning person, like getting up when the roosters are crowing and the sun is just barely peeking over the horizon. Early risers get to see sights that lazy bums don't get to see. I've been rewarded with one of those sights today.

I'm sitting on a little bench next to a water fountain in the park; the trees casting shade overtop my head and the fresh air feeling good in my lungs. The playground is laid out below me on the crest of the hill, and so many little children are busy having fun down there. My Little Red is down there now, her momma treating her to some fun since it ain't a school day. All flaming red hair and freckled cheeks, she's busy swinging just as high as she can on the swing set. Looks like she wants to touch the sky...

Her momma's busy chattering on her cell phone some distance away, not paying much attention to her little daughter. That's just fine with me. That's pretty damn perfect, matter of fact. I'm munching on my breakfast sandwich and keeping my eyes open. Today might be the day. The hour might be drawing near.

My mail sits on the bench beside me, and finally I decide to leaf through it while still watching Little Red out of the corner of my eye. Mostly just the same old junk I'm used to getting. Advertisements for Food Mart, letters offering me new car insurance and fancy credit cards, couple bills too.

A folded piece of paper slides out of the junk and lands in my lap. I pick it up, puzzling over it for a moment. It's totally blank, no stamp or return address or nothin' like that. What the hell is up with that?

I unfold...and I begin to read.

"You've been naughty, Edgar.

You've been a very bad boy for a very long time.

So many lives extinguished because of you, so much suffering inflicted by those fat, crude hands of yours. Hell's got a VIP section...and you're definitely on the list, big guy.

Congrats!

We know, Edgar.

We know everything.

At midnight you'll come to the place where the toads chirp and the bog water gurgles. You know it well. We'll talk this thing over. There is so much to discuss...

If you don't come, this goes public.

We'll be seeing you."

-The One That Lived

My eyes are bulging in my sockets. My lips are pressed down hard against my teeth, my entire mouth a thin white line. There's a hurricane raging inside of me. My emotions are caught in the hurricane, the rage and the confusion and the shock all swirling together.

I crumple the note up into one fist. This ain't gonna be such a good day after all.

14

Jack 2.0

I'm perched high in another sycamore in the park, Verminort and I gazing out across the rolling green hills. We watch as Edgar reads the note on the bench. We watch as he rises, his breakfast sandwich all but forgotten. We watch the big mastodon of a man trudge back up the hill towards the parking lot.

Even from so high up his face looks to be just simmering with rage, a reddish flush riding high on his fleshy cheeks. His lips are pushed out, looking almost bratty. His fists are clenched and they remain that way for the duration of his walk back to the tow truck.

As he nears the truck one of those meaty fists lashes out and a stiff right cross connects with a side view mirror, breaking it off completely and shattering the glass. He flexes that ham of a fist and then curls the fingers right back up again, the little glass particles in his knuckles seeming not to bother him even one bit.

"I'd say he got the message. Poor, innocent mirror..."

"Seems like we did a pretty good job of pissing him off."

"That's good, roomie. We want him angry. We want him fucking FURIOUS. If he's pissed he'll also be sloppy. We want him off his game, totally unsure of where to look or what to do. Edgar's never been called out like this before. We've shattered his sense of safety...and now we use that against him."

Malencourt is already spinning the tow truck around in the parking lot, the tires screeching and exhaust smoke pluming upwards.

"What's the next step?"

"We prepare for our little midnight meeting. That's the next step."

"Do you think he'll really come?"

"He'll come. He's pissed...and he has too much to lose. We just have to make sure we're ready for him when he gets there..."

***

It's musty in the derelict box factory, the stink of old cardboard seeming to infect the air itself. Verminort is working our body almost preternaturally fast, pulling iron nails from the walls and stripping electrical wires and lugging old propane tanks all over the place. I've taken a backseat while he does this, simply watching the demon as he utilizes my hands to construct trap after trap.

If there's anyone I would entrust to build innovative torture devices out of old, discarded junk...it's definitely Verminort.

The plan is to lure Edgar here after dark, the big man still fuming from the contents of the note. We want him to blunder in like a raging bull, the traps doing most of the work in dismantling him before we move in to finish off Greyfield's monster once and for all.

I'm looking forward to getting up close and personal with Edgar Malencourt. This better work...

15

Edgar

I'm driving down a forgotten highway that don't get much use anymore now that construction has finished on that fancy new interstate. My hands are very tight on the wheel and my eyes are wide open, bloodshot and twitchy. I don't dare blink.

The side view mirror's hanging onto the side of the truck with nothing but a few pieces of twisted metal to keep it connected. It keeps on rattling against the door and that's starting to really unnerve me. Everything about this clusterfuck of a day is starting to unravel me, the good mood I woke up with this morning laid to tatters by that SHIT-WHORE of a note...

Who wrote me that? Who could know those things?

It ain't the cops. If it was the cops, they'd have me in shackles already. They'd have cruisers tailing me and sirens blazing and roadblocks set up all over Greyfield.

Who does that leave, then? Don't make no god damn sense. I've been so careful. I've cleaned up my messes and I've given all my neighbors and customers that big fake smile that always seems to do the trick. Nobody can know about the children. Nobody can know about Sue. Nobody can know about my *sweet treats*...

There's a sound in the truck. It ain't the radio, I got that turned off. It's high-pitched and torn, sounding like some dangerous animal locked up in a furnace and screaming while it burns. I think I know what it is now. I'm sure I know.

It's coming from my own vocal cords.

The anger has turned my blood to acid and the scream just goes on and on, all the rage and frustration bleeding together into one. I yank the wheel to the side and guide the truck over onto the road's shoulder, dust pluming up all around me as I bring the vehicle to a screeching stop.

I open the door and get out, proceeding to head out to the back of the truck. The highway remains desolate. Utility poles line the road and power lines strum with electricity overtop my head. A few crows roost on these lines while cawing at each other. They are my only witnesses.

There's a special, secret toolbox in the back of the truck. It's metallic silver in color and it holds a whole different person inside of it. There ain't nothin of Edgar Malencourt in this box.

Not a man of flesh and blood and addictions and troubles.

Anguish lives in this box.

I open the lid and look within, my fingers caressing the items inside. I gaze at my box cutter, my propane torch, my screwdrivers and my pliers. So many tools, so much capacity for hurt. The tools of Anguish. There's the welder's mask too, the mask to hide me away. The face of Anguish.

Whoever wrote that note wants me to show up at that old box factory in the swamplands. It's the place where I took the last one, a place I know by heart. I don't know what waits for me there. I don't got the slightest fuckin' clue of what to expect.

That don't matter much to me. I don't like being exposed. I don't like being called out. All the eyes of Greyfield do nothing but see, but all the eyes of Greyfield ain't supposed to see me.

The sun is setting and midnight is just a few hours away.

Anguish does his best work after sundown.

16

Jack 2.0

My heartbeat is very loud in the silent vastness of the box factory. The thump of it reverberates through my ears and becomes like the ticking of a clock. There is no fear in the quickened pace of my heart, only anticipation. Verminort is deathly still inside of my head. I can feel him in there though—crouched and ready—a demonic missile just waiting to be fired. The body we both inhabit is crouched on a steel girder high up in the rafters. We're draped in shadow, ever watchful.

The cracked Avengers wristwatch I'm wearing has taken a beating but it still keeps time okay. I spare it a glance now, marking the hour as 11:59 pm. Minutes away from the fateful meeting with my tormentor, the murderer of countless innocent children.

I'm ready for him. I've never been more ready for anything else in my entire brief life on this planet. Another thump of the heart, another tick of the minute hand.

It's midnight now...and the monster of Greyfield is punctual. The back door opens far across the open floor of the factory and his enormous silhouette is there in the doorframe, moonlight giving him an ethereal shroud. He wears drab brown coveralls and that emotionless welder's mask covers his face. He takes a step inside and I hear the jangling of the metal instruments on his tool belt. I've felt the bite of almost every hideous tool in his arsenal...and the memories stir my hatred even more.

He is cautious. His head turns from side to side, scoping out his surroundings. The stink of him curls into my nostrils—all body odor and motor oil—the stench of a grotesque grease monkey.

Now we wait. We wait for him to stumble into one of the little surprises we've labored over for him. Edgar Malencourt is instinctually careful—a predator that has learned from hunt after hunt—but he's not an intelligent man. The brute has a certain low cunning but he knows nothing of finesse. That is the character flaw we're banking on...

He's stalking through the narrow corridors, weaving between dusty assembly lines and archaic machinery. Edgar is all hunched shoulders, his hands clenching and unclenching at his sides. He rounds a corner and a loud SNAP sound pierces through the silence of the box factory...followed by a piggish squeal of pain.

The homemade bear trap was rudimentary, just a triggering mechanism and metal blades from an old paper shredder, but it did the trick. Verminort's own design, and I can already smell the blood dripping down Edgar's log-sized leg.

He struggles and claws at the leg of his coveralls, his tools jangling loudly as he bends forward over his bulbous stomach.

His breathing is loud and practically asthmatic, some burly animal reacting to a less than comfortable situation.

He's trapped, finally vulnerable. Verminort breaks his silence in the house that is my skull.

"Let's go say hello..."

***

We flip downward gracefully and land in the narrow aisle several yards away from the trapped Malencourt. His struggles immediately cease, the welder's mask tilting upwards as he notices the new arrival standing in front of him. Little droplets of blood trickle down from the twisted metal teeth embedded in the meat of his calf muscle. He stares, his head cocking to the side. I can't see his face but his body language shows me obvious bewilderment.

"Nice to see you again, Edgar."

His ham-sized fists clench at the sound of his own name.

"Remember me?"

He says nothing for several moments. When his voice finally drifts out from behind the mask it's hollow and toneless. It's the first time I've ever heard him speak.

"You're dead," said Malencourt, the barest hint of disbelief in his voice. "Killed you. Got little pieces of you in a jar..."

52

"Afraid not, Edgar. I'm very much alive...I've even been given an upgrade since the last time we met. Let me show you..."

Verminort is working his magic inside of me, turning my body backwards and contorting my spinal cord forward until my hands and feet hit the floor, my body splayed out unnaturally in a totally inhuman form. I begin to spider-walk across the floor towards Malencourt, my head weaving from side to side as I crawl on the tips of my toes and the tips of my extended fingers. Demonic possession is great for the joints...flexibility in particular.

Finally something registers in the voice of Malencourt, something I've desperately wanted to hear. It's low and confused, but it's there, stripped of all false pretenses. It's fear.

"What the fuck kinda thing are you?"

He begins to claw and dig at his pant's leg again, trying to pull the trap from his flesh.

"Stay the fuck back...I'll kill you again, devil boy. Don't get near me..."

I smile, my lips stretching and stretching, my teeth chattering as I spider-walk closer and closer.

"Too late for that, Edgar. There are things you've done in life...things that have consequences. This is the trial of Mr. Malencourt..."

My hand drifts closer, my back arching and my joints cracking.

"I am your judge."

He's grunting with exertion, using his meaty fingers to pry at the sides of the trap.

"I am your jury."

I'm inches away from him now, so close that I can see the sweat cutting through the grease stains on his flabby bare arms.

"I am your motherfuckin' executioner."

I'm poised, ready to leap directly into his face with teeth and fingernails...and at the exact same moment he uses his brute strength to force the trap open and extract his foot from the twisted metal. He's deceptively quick for a big man, the box cutter already in his hand before I can even react. He lurches forward and slashes at me and I'm just barely able to dodge backwards. He keeps coming, charging forward and swinging his arm from side to side, the box cutter blade slicing through thin air directly in front of my face. I cartwheel backwards, leaping and ducking and dodging.

The chase takes us around the corner and he pulls a screwdriver from his tool belt and stabs it downward, aiming for my head, but I'm able to dart to the left just in time. The screwdriver blade buries itself in a wooden table and Edgar blunders into another tripwire, this one unleashing the rope holding a swinging pendulum covered in shattered glass.

The pendulum swings downward and CRASHES into Malencourt, knocking him violently to the side, several little lacerations opened up along his left arm and his ribs. A tattered piece of his coveralls hangs downward, the flesh of his saggy side torn and impaled by little shards of broken bottles. Somehow the giant keeps his feet, his grunt of pain overshadowed only by the rising anger inside of him.

I flip atop a large barrel and leap forwards for the kill, but a massive fist catches me square in the face and knocks me right out of the sky. I fall across a table, barely just landing before a hand digs into my t-shirt and that same fist crashes down over and over again against my face and stomach, little shockwaves of pain hitting me hard.

If I was still just a twelve year old boy I'd likely be unconscious by now but the whirling presence of Verminort keeps me in the fight, the demon taking control and scraping up some crumbling tile pieces only to toss the mixture directly into Edgar's eyes. Malencourt stumbles back blindly and I regain my footing and send a brutal punt of a kick directly into his throat, causing him to stumble further down the aisle while choking and sputtering for breath. I spin around the giant and drive a sharp uppercut into his ribs but I'm immediately met by a slash of the box cutter. A hot little wound opens along my lower abdomen and I have to clamp a hand against it to keep the blood from flowing freely.

I'm so distracted by the wound that I don't even notice when Malencourt's strong hands wrap around my throat and push me up against the concrete wall, lifting me up off my feet. His thumbs dig deeply into my neck as he attempts to strangle me.

My sight grows dim, the voice of Verminort sounding panicked and distant in my head.

"Get back in the game, Jack! Stay with me!"

Edgar presses the welder's mask close to my slackening face, his grip tightening even more.

"Die again, little devil boy. Die for me..."

These words, so callous and foul, seem to burn in my ears. My desire for vengeance starts to force new life into my weakening limbs. The infernal will of Verminort strengthens the vengeance, empowering it and making it grow. My eyes blaze wide, black and vacant gulfs...and simply the sight of them makes Edgar's grip momentarily falter.

"You first."

My head darts forward and I thrust my chin upwards, knocking the welder's mask off of Edgar's face. He scrambles for it with one hand while keeping the other locked around my throat...and I take that moment to crane my neck forward and clamp my teeth securely around the meat of Edgar's ear. I bite down as hard as I possibly can; tearing and sawing at the flesh, blood pumping into my mouth and down my throat, Edgar's agonized screams ringing in my ears. I don't stop biting until the entire lump of ruined flesh comes off on my tongue...and then I swallow it whole.

Malencourt stumbles backward, his hand clamped across the mangled crater where his ear used to be. His eyes look wild and desperate, his screams full of such beautiful suffering.

Verminort assumes control once again and leaps up onto the assembly line only to run forward and piston a dropkick into Edgar's chest, knocking the man directly into another carefully placed tripwire. This is the best tripwire of all...the trap I've been waiting for.

A splash of lighter fluid bursts forward out of a funnel on one side of Edgar and a burst of flame erupts from a propane tank on the other side of him. The lighter fluid only saturates his right arm and shoulder, but that part of him immediately takes to the flame. The fire sizzles across his arm, the monster of Greyfield actually braying with pain now, swinging his meaty limb from side to side in an effort to extinguish the flames.

He retreats, a burning ball of fat man charging past old equipment and knocking down stacks of boxes before slamming into an emergency exit door and running off into the swamplands. I'm about to give chase but a sharp pain from my lower abdomen almost knocks me off my feet, causing me to lean back against a rusted compactor.

My hand reaches down to touch the wound and when I bring it up my fingertips are very wet and very red.

"We're hurt, Jack. We can't finish him like this. Let me take the lead..."

I drift off into the nether regions of my mind where the pain is numb and unimportant, Verminort controlling my body and maintaining a staggered pace towards the front door of the factory. I notice him pick up a metal paperweight from a rotten office desk before stumbling into the warm night air.

I let my thoughts fade; I let my demon lead us into retreat.

It wasn't supposed to be like this.

I vaguely hear the sounds of a manhole being uncovered and I feel the sensation of our body descending down into the sewer system. It's all distant.

This wasn't supposed to happen...

I was supposed to finish it.

17

Edgar

It's hot. It's too damn hot. Gotta get away from the heat. I'm melting. My skin is sloughing off and melting away. It burns so much. It hurts so much. Ain't never felt nothin' like this before.

I ain't supposed to feel the hurt.

Anguish gives the hurt, he don't get it.

There's smoke in my eyes and I can't see shit. There are pieces of glass sticking outta me. I can't hear nothin' outta my ear but I can feel blood spurting out of the hole where it used to be. It's awful. I'm running and I'm running but there's smoke in my eyes and blood on my face and fire on my flesh and HOW THE FUCK DID THIS HAPPEN TO ME???

I stumble and see just the slightest glimmer of moonlight on that stinky bog water and I plunge into it like a man in the desert coming across the sweetest water he's ever seen. The splash sends toads hopping away and snakes slithering for safety, a wave of fetid water passing across the surface. There's a horrible sizzling sound as the flames along my arm and shoulder finally die in the stagnant wetness.

I'm in a shallow part of the bog and I roll onto my back and just let myself float there, gritting my teeth against the various levels of hurt that I'm suffering through. My big body ain't never felt nothin' like this before. Anguish wasn't made for this. I'm built to stab and cut and smash, I ain't built to face this kinda treatment.

The murky water oozes around my lacerations and my burns, giving me just the slightest comfort. Extremely minimal comfort that does very little to mute the pain that's scorching through my soul. My eyes catch on the moon, the pale light shining down on me as I lie here, brought down as low as a man can possibly be. I focus on the moon. I stare at the craters, the torn and ragged surface of that distant moon.

The anger returns. It burns with the fury of the flames that enveloped me. It's hot and it's nasty...but I like this kinda heat.

I'm gonna tear craters into that devil boy's face until it looks just like the moon. I'm gonna split it open and rip him up until he's ragged...just like the moon high in that black ol' sky.

He don't get to hurt me like this...no one does.

I dunno what kinda weird occult shit spat that devil boy back up outta the shadows of death...but I'm gonna send him back where he came from. This ain't over. This...is far from done.

My smile is a little rotten from the lollipops and there's still blood on my teeth, but I smile my biggest and brightest grin up at that cratered moon. I move my arms silently through the water, sending ripples across the swamplands. The ripples look like the wings of an angel taking flight. That's what I'll be for this devil boy...an angel rising from the swamplands to sink holy spears into his black little heart.

I ain't dead.

Anguish lives.

18

Jack 2.0

I'm caught in the heart of delirium. Reality and fantasy blend together, spliced into one haunting visual experience. I see flashes of firelight from a campfire. I see the mucky walls of a sewer corridor. There's the swirling black and red cloud that is the essence of Verminort, those inky black rodent eyes staring deeply into my core. Heavy feet stomp through my mind and there stands the mammoth that is Malencourt, box cutter slashing through the air as he howls like a wounded wolf.

There's my mother fixing me a grilled cheese sandwich and asking me how school went today. There's me sitting in my dark room with only the light from my terrarium shining, my toads hopping around inside and snapping up crickets with long tongues. There's the fire, crackling and warm against my face. Verminort's voice cuts through the fever, sounding warped and far away.

"We have to stop the bleeding, Jack. Bite down on this..."

Something is thrust into my mouth. Tastes like old wood, very stale. I watch my own hand reaching out towards the fire but I'm not in control of it. There's a metal paperweight held against the flames, one side of it growing molten and hot. I'm transfixed by the dull gray of the metal becoming a vibrant orange.

"This is gonna hurt. It won't hurt like Hell, nothing hurts that bad...but it's still gonna suck..."

I barely hear this. There's a battalion of rats watching us from the pipes lining the ceiling, standing vigil to the scene below them. They twitch their little noses, whiskers flicking. I try to count them but my head starts to feel muggy again and I lose count. The remembered sounds of the factory return, traps snapping and blood dripping. The flaming form of the fat man dances through my fever dreams, twirling and twirling like a ballerina, his eyes staring at me with such naked hate.

And then something incredibly hot touches my belly and a muffled scream tears through my vocal cords around the stick between my teeth, the sound so loud and long that it dries out every bit of saliva in my mouth. I spare a glance down at my wound just as my hand draws the paperweight away, the flesh freshly cauterized and the bleeding nonexistent. The brand is a perfect square of wavering pain and I barely have time to examine it before I collapse back downward with exhaustion.

"Rest now. We have to heal, Jack. Remember, this body is confined to the laws of the Earthly plane. There's no dark magic I'm privy to that will make us all better. Only time will do that."

My teeth unclench and the chunk of wood falls out of my mouth, rolling across the fetid floor of the sewer. Verminort has assumed control, limping across the corridor to attach an old blanket to both sections of the wall, creating a makeshift hammock that hangs high above the running waste below.

My body sinks into this hammock and it feels like the best bed I've ever laid on in my entire lifetime. I watch my hand moving again, the demon giving it motion and grinding up a piece of some unknown root into brittle. Verminort slimes this root-paste across my gums and into my mouth. I swallow with some effort. It tastes mildly sweet, almost pleasant.

"For the pain. Dr. Verminort's orders..."

I barely manage a weak whisper.

"Shouldn't you be inflicting pain instead of treating it, demon?"

Verminort laughs in my head, a soft chattering of merriment.

"Good to know your sarcasm isn't injured, roomie. Look at it this way...when it comes to this precious body we share, I'm all about preventive maintenance."

I want to say more but I'm already drifting away, the fever carrying me back into colorful delusions.

The rats chatter and scurry overhead.

They serenade me off to broken sleep.

19

Edgar

This little upstairs bathroom feels so damn cramped, no room for a big-boned man to take care of himself. Gotta lean down low to see my own face in the mirror. I'm finishing up the stitching on the remnants of my ear, the needle passing through flesh and closing the hole with black thread.

There still ain't no sound from that hole. The eardrum is punctured and it won't never be right again. Got my arm and shoulder slathered up real good with petroleum jelly and that cools the burns a little, but they still hurt fiercely.

I'm been popping painkillers like skittles. Takes a lot of them to numb all the hurt I've been forced to feel. He fucked me up good, that devil boy. He fucked me up worse than I've ever been fucked up in all my days. Anguish ain't never gonna forget that. The flames that touched my flesh, the crunch of teeth that took away half my hearing, the little pieces of broken bottle I got sticking outta my side…every memory is fresh fuel for the fury.

I pick up the metal tongs now and carefully use them to extract pieces of broken glass outta my side. I got me a few rolls of belly meat that hang low so I gotta pick those up to get at the glass. This motherfuckin' bathroom too damn small…making me suffer more. I'm tempted to beat my fists against the fuckin' walls til they crumble into dust, til I got me some room to breathe.

I gotta cool down, though. I'm banged up and I ain't at my best. Little bloody holes mark my side and I slather some Neosporin on them, proceeding to bandage them up best I can with some old gauze from the medicine cabinet.

Gotta rest up for a few days and take it easy. Anguish needs time to regroup, to come back stronger. Nobody fucks me up like this. Cut that devil boy up pretty good with the box cutter…but didn't cut him up good enough to do the job permanently. He might have already sacrificed a goat or somethin and cast a spell to fix up that gut wound. I gotta be on my guard.

Soon as I'm feeling better I'm gonna find him. I'm gonna hunt him and sniff every dark, lonely place in Greyfield til I smell the stink of his little brimstone body. And then...I'm gonna smash him and crush him and brutalize him til he's just bloody pulp, and I'm gonna put that pulp into the biggest jar I can find.

He'll be the *sweetest devil treat* ever, the centerpiece of my collection. I'm saving him a spot right up on the top shelf.

But now I'm hurting and I need me some comfort.

Think I'll go lay in the bed with Sue for awhile...

20

Jack 2.0

It's been four days now. The fever broke on the third day, but I'm still weak. The wound is slowly but surely healing, Verminort occasionally rubbing some of that root-paste into the torn flesh to speed up the process. We collect the rain water that pours in through the gutters in an old plastic bottle and that is what we use to hydrate our shared body. Each night Verminort calls to a rat and the rat comes, sacrificing itself for our continued survival. Four days of eating roasted rats...I'm actually starting to enjoy the taste of them.

It's boring down here in the depths of the sewer waiting for my body to heal. I wonder about Malencourt and where he is right now. I wonder about what kind of state he's in. I sincerely hope he burned to death outside the box factory but something in my heart tells me that the monster of Greyfield was not so easily vanquished. I can still feel him out there somewhere, a walking sickness infecting the town itself.

I use a long stick to poke at the flames of the campfire, watching the embers float through the air. The rain patters on the streets above our head. I think about my mother. I think about how worried she must be. Surely she thinks I'm dead and gone now.

"You seem glum, roomie..."

"I miss my mother."

"Ah. Why do you miss her?"

The question perplexes me.

"I miss her because she's my mother. I love her."

"Love. I know nothing of love, Jack. I've heard the tales and the stories of human love. There are some souls in Hell that have been there for centuries and still they howl for those they love. They are damned, forgotten...but still they love."

The demon grows quiet in my head. He seems almost contemplative.

"Why?"

"It's a part of who we are, Verminort. It's what makes us human. If there is love...there will always be hope."

The demon remains silent for awhile. He seems to have no reply for this, no understanding of the statement.

"Do you love your father as well?"

"I don't know my father. He left right after I was born. I've never seen a picture of him. I don't even know his name..."

I examine my own knuckles for a moment, crusted over with old blood and scabs from the fight in the box factory.

"Do you have a family?"

"Yes."

"Tell me about them."

"It is hard for me to describe the indescribable. My mother is what we call a Breeder in Hell, a massive glob of teats and teeth with a vaginal opening to release the brood-sac. She holds no significance to me. These Breeders float through the circles of Hell and drop their brood-sacs and then float on, never again to be recognized by their children. The vastness of Hell is beyond your understanding, roomie. It is worlds overtopped with worlds, all of them smeared in scum and ruin."

Verminort pauses, the flames dancing in front of the eyes we both look out from.

"I had a little over six thousand brothers and sisters at the moment of my hatching from the brood-sac. Hell is survival, Jack. You survive by whatever means necessary. My brothers and sisters and I cannibalized each other, rending flesh and tissue until only four of us remained. We were exhausted then and rather than continue the fight we went our separate ways. I've not seen them since."

"That sounds...horrible. Didn't you mention your father awhile back?"

"Oh yeah, precious papa. I crawled across the thirteenth circle after surviving the blood-feast of my birth and came across my father torturing John Wayne Gacy. If I remember correctly he was sticking scorpions decorated in clown greasepaint up Gacy's ass. My dad is old school, all cloven hooves and phallic horns. Naturally I did what any son would do...I went in for the hug."

"How'd that go?"

"Not so great. He punted me into a pit of meat-maggots. Think I told you that part of the story already. He considered me the runt of the litter. After that…I was pretty much on my own. Unwanted and alone, Hell's ultimate loser."

My teeth grit, my fists clenching just slightly in front of the campfire. Verminort's anger manifests itself through my own body. It feels especially strange.

"I vowed that day to make something of myself despite my less than fortunate situation. The greatest triumph for a demon, big or small, great or nameless…is to find and secure flesh. It is the highest accomplishment to enter a body on the Earthly plane. I've done that, Jack. Thanks to your help and permission…I've felt the sublime melding of essence and flesh."

My fists unclench and my jaw relaxes. I feel the anger fading from the house that is my skull.

"But enough about our daddy issues and all that crap, Jack. We still have unfinished business to conduct together. Our goal now is to heal so that we'll be strong enough to finish what we started."

"Fair enough."

There's something eating at me though, a question that's been circling through my mind ever since I gave this demon access to my body. It's a cosmic question, one that every man and woman likely asks at some point in their lives.

"There's obviously a Hell populated by demons and tortured souls, you've proven that to me, so doesn't that mean that there has to be an opposing force, Verminort?"

The demon tenses up in my head, seeming to suspect where this conversation is going.

"Doesn't that mean…there's a God?"

My lips immediately part and Verminort spits into the fire.

"Yuck. Gross. I hate that G-word, Jack. Makes me wanna scrub myself with a brillo pad. If there is such an entity—a g-o-d—I'm ignorant to all details of him or her. I was born in Hell and I know only of the infernal. The very topic of the G-word is banned in Hell, punishable by ritualistic disembowelment and then hanging by your own entrails."

Verminort brings my hand down and scrapes it across the floor of the sewer, bringing up some dust and allowing it to slip through the cracks in my fingers.

"But since we're not in Hell right now, I'll tell you this much. There are stories and legends. Most of those stories come from Lu—The Devil, Old Scratch, Lucifer Morningstar—when he's around. He rarely stays at home, prefers to walk the Earthly plane in one form or another, but when he is in Hell, his tales tend to spread. The stories bespeak of a place where light is forever and songs are always sung and creatures with white wings fly and fly. The stories tell of an ancient war and Lu's fall...his banishment from that place of light."

"That place sounds awesome."

"You kidding me? Sounds like a boring shithole. And who needs constant light? How the fuck are you supposed to nap with some divine nightlight shining in your face all the time? Count me out, roomie. Need my beauty sleep..."

I can't help but shake my head, chuckling slightly in the dankness of the sewer.

"So negative."

"Yeah, well I'm also honest, Jack. Besides...there's no light to be found in the work we have yet to do. It's dark, gritty work. The business of death always is."

"On that...we agree."

21

Edgar

I'm pounding sixteen-penny nails into a heavy bedpost I found up in the attic. The hammer falls hard, the sound of metal hitting metal heard only by my one good ear. My strength ain't what it once was and sometimes my aim with the hammer ain't true. It's been two weeks since the box factory and the devil boy. Things been falling apart since then.

Ear-hole didn't heal right. Got a powerful infection in it and greedy green flies been buzzing around it wherever I go, giving me no peace. Sometimes I gotta wipe the yellowish pus away from it because it's always dripping down my cheek.

Hurts bad.

My arm is going dead. The burns done cracked open wide, showing red viscera inside. There's the stink of rot clinging to that arm and parts of it are going black, some pieces starting to drop off. Necrotic tissue, I think it's called. Dunno rightly when the gangrene set in, but it's been there a few days now. Time has gotten all fuzzy in my head, hard to focus on stuff.

I can smell myself rotting.

I've been popping them painkillers all the time now. Don't care much if they kill me. Might be better if they did. Thought about going to the hospital but it wouldn't do nothin but open the jar to questions that I can't answer. Too late now. Too far gone.

I'm in the pantry using the stool to hammer nails into this bedpost. My *sweet treats* surround me, giving me the boost I need to finish my work. I'm desperate to absorb the power of the jars before ol' Edgar Malencourt kicks the bucket for good.

That's what's gonna happen. I've come to accept it.

I'm a dead man walking and soon the rot gonna be all through me. Already feel brain-sick, kinda like one of them mad cows that just wants to snort and kick and froth at the mouth. Don't got a whole lotta time left.

There's one last thing I gotta do before I go into the ground.

I gotta find that devil boy. I gotta rip him into small pieces and pull his heart outta his chest. I gotta smash him to bloody bits with this new toy and I gotta stick what is left in a jar.

My new toy is finished. I raise it up and examine it, liking the look of all those sharp nails jutting out from the head of the bedpost. It's a damn good club for bashing in devil boy brains.

Lost the welder's mask during the fight. That face of Anguish is gone forever. I'm sad to see it go. I approach a special drawer in the pantry now and open it up wide. Inside is the first face of Anguish. It's the origin of my work, the first mask I ever put on my face and the first time I ever gave a child the hurt. The boy's name was Billy. His jar sits on the top shelf now, his severed big toe floating in formaldehyde.

I bring the mask up into my hands, looking down into the eyeholes. I stitched it together from an old tan leather jacket with white twine to hold it together. There's a red lipstick frown drawn across the mouth and the number ten smeared across the forehead.

I got the idea for that from those posters you see in the doctor's office, the ones that ask "how bad is your pain on a scale from zero to ten?" I remember the zero always had a smiley face above it...but the ten always had that miserable frown sittin' on top. It inspired me.

Anguish don't never settle for giving just a little bit of hurt on the zero to ten scale.

He don't give you a three or a four, because then you might still be smiling.

He don't even settle for a six or a seven, because even though you're uncomfortable, you ain't truly lost in the hurt.

Anguish ain't satisfied until his victim is feeling an absolute motherfuckin' ten on the pain scale. It's gotta be the worst. It's gotta be that big, saggy frown face. It was the last expression on little Billy's face after I cranked the pain up to ten and sent him off to the afterlife.

I pull the mask on now, letting the memories of my first victim slither through my heart and my soul. I've gained a little weight and lost an ear since then, but the first face of Anguish seems to fit just as snug as ever. I feel the need growing inside me again, the desire to give the hurt, overriding my own hurt for just a few moments.

I'm gonna find that fuckin' devil boy before I die and take him along for the ride with me.

I'm gonna give him the ten that he deserves.

22

Gathering Storm

For an entire week light rain has been falling in Greyfield. There's a breeze cutting through the July air, pleasant and cool, but full of energy from the Atlantic. Many of the town's old folks grow somber, some of them sitting in rocking chairs on the porches of homes they've lived in and will die in, having never had the desire to leave the familiarity of the Mountain State. They say there's a storm coming. It's a feeling in their bones, old Appalachian intuition. They say they remember the days when the wind tore trees from the ground like they were mere toothpicks. They talk of thunder that rattles the earth and lightning that damn near blinds.

The old storms from the old years, rare and etched into the realm of legend. The bygone days when the flood waters ran freely through Harpers Ferry and the barns burned brightly in Rust Valley, scorched by bolts from the angry sky.

The wind doesn't lie.

An old man sits in a wheelchair in his backyard, the wilderness encroaching on all sides and a little babbling brook cutting through his property. Flocks of blackbirds fly overhead, swirling and swirling through the sky, seeming perturbed. They fly off to the west, seeking safe haven. The old man watches them go, his still keen eyes—the palest blue—shining in the sun.

His little blonde grandchildren play in the yard near the brook with battered toy soldiers, the same toy soldiers the old man once played with in his youth. He keeps a close eye on the boys. He still reads the newspaper and has heard all the talk about the missing children in Greyfield. You can't be too careful these days.

He is Abel Campbell—the last centenarian in this little slice of West Virginia—and at 103 years old he's still as sharp in body and mind as the pocket knife he's using to whittle with. He knows the taste of ocean air in his lungs even this far inland. He's seen the birds and the animals act strangely before when changes occur in barometric pressure. The wrinkles on his face are so tremendously deep, his features carved by the decades. His eyes are wise and full of secrets seen in these hills, a lifetime of stories locked behind his gaze.

He remembers the night when he was still a young husband with a young and beautiful wife, seven children playing and laughing near the hearth in the old home place. He went out to use the outhouse and there on the roof of it stood a big mountain cat with a pelt as black as midnight. The eyes glowed yellow and the mountain cat screamed. He'll never forget the sound it made. It was like the shriek of a dying woman. It vanished into the woods after that, leaving him there with a hammering heart.

He remembers the little cabin he used to visit during hunting trips with his old friends. He remembers the night when he was awoken by the sound of chunks of wood from the pile being thrown against the front door. He stormed out and opened the door, seeing the small pile of cut wood at his feet. There was nothing and no one outside, the silence broken only by the chirping of crickets. He slept not a wink that night because something kept throwing that wood at his door, but each time he went to check, he was greeted by nothing at all.

There are secret, unexplainable things in the Appalachians.

There are strange things in the hills that no man ever forgets when he encounters them.

He remembers the storms best of all.

The great, cataclysmic storms that tore through the towns of men like they were nothing but anthills to be stomped on. He remembers whole houses smashed to pieces and livestock flung up into the air and impaled on the sharp branches of trees. One such storm took hold of him when he rode his bicycle back home with a loaf of bread in the basket for his family. It carried him high and spun him round and round, and only by some stark miracle was he set back down upon the road again, still alive to tell the tale. He never did recover his loaf of bread.

Something is coming now. Old Abel can practically taste it when he sticks out his tongue to catch a few light raindrops.

It'll be bad. It'll be destructive. Perhaps it will be the worst storm of all...

The darkening clouds on the horizon look ominous above the mountains, black and full of bad intentions. Old Abel begins pushing his wheelchair towards the house, calling out to his grandchildren as he goes.

"Come on in, boys."

The little ones look up, their toy soldiers momentarily forgotten.

"There's a storm coming."

The boys gather up their toy soldiers and spare one final glance at the clouds above the mountains. The distant, faraway boom of thunder makes them run for the door just a little bit faster.

23

Jack 2.0

Black clouds hover over downtown Greyfield. I hear the jingling of wind chimes somewhere in the distance. A wicked storm is gathering, born of nature's everlasting fury. I walk with the coming storm, my vengeance warming my heart. The light rain has soaked my hair down against my brow, little droplets cutting through the grime smeared across my face. I catch a glimpse of that face in the shop window of Panhandle Sporting Goods. My features are aged far beyond that of a normal twelve year old, my eyes twinkling with the ferocity of my inner demon and the old soul of a boy forced to grow up far too quickly.

We've left the sewer behind for good, the wound on my abdomen pink and closed with freshly healed tissue. I feel strong. I feel capable. I feel ready to finish the job that I started.

I stand silently before the shop window, the wind starting to pick up and pull at my wet clothes. We're watching a little white mouse crawl along a wire on the inside of the window. The wire leads to the shop's alarm system, the plastic box set into the wall with a blinking digital readout. The albino mouse reaches the end of the wire and looks back at us, little pink eyes seeming almost to question. Verminort answers the look with a single word.

"*Chew.*"

The mouse complies, starting to lay into the wire with those sharp little teeth. The wire's casing is shredded and then the mouse starts on the exposed silver wires. There's a little crackle of electricity and a jolt seems to pass through the mouse as the alarm system shorts out. The mouse's little body becomes still and falls down to the floor, a faintly smoking critter corpse.

"*Appreciate the sacrifice, little buddy.*"

I pull my soaked t-shirt up over my head and wrap it around my fist, proceeding to smash knuckles through the shop's glass door. There's a hollow shattering as the glass breaks, but no alarm follows the forced entry. My hand snakes down to the knob and opens the door from the inside, my demon and I entering and shaking off some of the rain. A little puddle forms around our shoes as we step deeper into the empty shop.

I look around at the confines, seeing the vast arsenal presented to me. I'll make use of it. This will be my last stand. My final opportunity to slay the monster of Greyfield.

We start exploring and grabbing, Verminort using one hand while I use the other. We're kids in a twisted candy store...and there are so many goodies that catch the eyes we share.

***

We stand before a full length mirror in the shop's restroom. A black Kevlar vest is wrapped securely around our torso, feeling both light and protective. Dark cargo pants cover our legs and steel toe combat boots adorn our feet. We slicked back our hair with rain water, two little curls reaching down across our forehead like twirling horns. How appropriate.

There's a machete in my right hand and a machete in my left, the blades carbon fiber and incredibly sharp. They feel good in my hands and I can't help but rotate them once before sheathing them across my back.

"Looking good, Rambo."

The voice comes from the left side of my mouth, a wicked little smirk pulling at the corner of my lips and an obsidian black eye glaring forward.

I respond from the right side of my body, still blue-eyed and taking in my own badass reflection.

"You're not so bad yourself."

Perfect duality.

We'll need each other if this is a fight we hope to win...

24

Edgar

So hot. World shimmers. I'm hot on the inside now. I'm stripped down to nothin' but some underpants but I'm still sweating like a greased hog. I was able to put the fire out that scorched my flesh but there ain't no putting out this fire inside of me. It's growing and the painkillers only dull the flames.

I've moved my little stool to the foyer facing the front door of the house. I've been sitting here, waiting and watching. I gotta believe the devil boy will come. It's my only chance to get him. I can't risk going out now, not in this sorry ass condition I'm in.

I'm falling apart.

Whole sections of my arm have turned a gooey black and there ain't no feeling in much of the flesh. It stinks like the grave. I can still move it up and down, but it don't feel quite right. It feels like a mushy piece of fruit that's been left out for too long, something gone bad.

Some of them flies got into my ear-hole when I was sleeping. They laid eggs in the festering wound. I can feel the newborn maggots squirming around in my head now. I can't hear em' on that side but I can feel the little worms squiggling around and eating their fill. They'll get to my brain soon. They'll gobble up my thoughts and my dreams.

The painkillers are keeping me upright, but not for much longer. The strength draining right outta me. It's gotta be soon. That no-good little cursed bastard from Hell better get here soon. I feel in my heart that he'll come. He wants me just like I want him. We are destined to come together.

My eyes are locked on that front door and I got a hold of my homemade club with the nails sticking outta it. I like the feel of that solid wood in my hands. It's comforting...and if the devil boy don't come, I'll just smash the head of the club into my own face until my life drips out onto the floor.

The TV is chattering and chirping from somewhere in the living room, a weatherman going on and on about some big tropical storm that's almost here. He keeps on saying stay indoors, seek immediate shelter, damage could be catastrophic. I can hear the wind picking up outside the walls of the house. It sounds powerful, getting stronger by the minute.

It's funny, though. I can't help but let out a big ol' belly laugh. What this weatherman don't know...is that the damage done to Edgar Malencourt is already pretty fuckin' catastrophic.

I'm broken, I'm bleeding, and I'm rotting to pieces.

I hear something that makes me forget all that. It's the sound of a window in the kitchen shattering. It's followed by the sound of light footsteps, getting closer and closer. I can smell the stink of brimstone. I search the shadows with my eyes, my grip on the club tightening.

I take up the leather mask from the table in the foyer and I pull it on for the last time. My face becomes the face of Anguish. My body becomes a vessel made purely to give the hurt. I am what the dictionaries call me, a sadist at heart.

This is where it ends...

Anguish rises.

The devil boy is here.

25

Convergence

The hulking monstrosity that is Malencourt glares across the foyer, his blubbery chest heaving with labored breathing. He lets the spiked club drag against the floor, actually leaning on it a bit. Jack stands about ten feet away in the doorway leading into the kitchen. The demon-infused boy has unsheathed the machetes from his back, his eyes locked on the monster of Greyfield that stands swaying in front of him.

The wind begins to howl outside the walls of House Malencourt. The light rain becomes a downpour, heavy and beating against the windows and the roof. The storm is no longer gathering, no longer gaining strength as it rages towards this little town in West Virginia. The time for waiting is over, the calm that preceded it finally at an end.

The storm is here.

Jack speaks first, raising his voice over the sound of the heavy rain and the shrieking wind.

"You've seen better days, Edgar..."

Malencourt replies with a grunt, nothing more. Flies buzz around the festering wound where his ear used to be, little tendrils of red infection crawling across the exposed parts of his face that the mask doesn't cover. His bad arm is black and sagging, a pulpy, putrefying appendage. Jack watches as the giant pulls a strand of barbwire from his filthy underpants and starts wrapping it around the deadened flesh of the arm, making a weapon of the limb. Edgar shows no signs of pain as he does this. The dead flesh of that arm seems beyond pain now...

Jack remains unimpressed. His eyes glimmer in the weak overhead light cast through the foyer, one iris a bright blue and the other an obsidian black. He and Verminort share the body at this moment, the two combined for the massive challenge that Malencourt presents.

"It's over for you, Edgar. You'll haunt this town no longer. You'll prey on the weak and the innocent no longer. The empire

77

that you've built here—this empire of bloodshed—finally crashes down on you tonight."

Edgar sways on his feet, proceeding to take just one shambling step closer to the boy. The spiked club drags across the floor behind him.

"Remember all the ones you've hurt, Malencourt. Think about how they suffered. Think about their tears and their horror and how they begged you for mercy. The fallen, you *piece of shit*. I'm here on their behalf just as much as my own."

Malencourt stops for a moment, cocking his head slightly to the left. A little drip of saliva runs out of the corner of his mouth and oozes down past the leather of the Anguish mask.

"Tonight you pay—in pounds of flesh and quarts of blood— you pay the fallen what you owe them."

Edgar lifts the club up from the floor, bringing it higher with the uncanny strength that still thrums through his good arm. The wind tears through the cracks and crevices of the old house, the bulb above Malencourt's head starting to flicker.

Finally the voice of Anguish is heard.

"The fallen…heh…"

Edgar and Jack stand so terribly close now, the tension seeming as thick as the black clouds in the sky outside. It's like those critical moments before a Wild West duel, both combatants attempting to gain the measure of the other. A meaty hand tightens on the spiked club and two small hands start to bring dual machetes up just a little higher.

"Go join em'."

A bloodthirsty roar follows this, Edgar making his shambling charge while raising the club up over his head. He swings high and hard, Jack barely managing to dodge the blow. The head of the spiked club smashes into the kitchen doorframe, shattering plaster and leaving a massive hole in the wall.

Edgar keeps coming, rotating the club around and sending a low swipe towards Jack's side, but Jack parries the attack with one of the machete blades. Nails screech against blade, the two coming dangerously close to each other before they push backwards and break the standoff. Jack makes several wild lunges with the machetes, hacking and slashing at Malencourt.

The big man is able to block most of these with the club, but one slash gets past his defenses and slices off a portion of his dead arm's bicep, a black hunk of rotting meat falling to the floor. Edgar doesn't seem to even notice, proceeding to simply backhand Jack across the mouth with that same hand, a little piece of barbwire catching him across the bottom lip and splitting it wide open. Jack stumbles backwards into the kitchen counter with fresh blood running down his chin. He leans over the sink and spits a glob of plasma down the drain, turning back to Edgar with a blood-stained grin smeared across his teeth.

Edgar runs forward and boxes the boy in, aiming a hard right cross at Jack's face. Jack ducks the gangrenous fist and the knuckles smash into a toaster, the little broken machine flying across the kitchen from the impact. Jack takes advantage of the moment and slices downward with one of the machetes, catching Edgar along the back of the thigh and leaving a ragged laceration along his flabby flesh. Edgar grunts in pain, spinning around to send a massive elbow into the top of Jack's chest. The Kevlar plates absorb most of the blow but Jack is still thrown backwards into the sink, the faucet digging into his upper back.

The two combatants come together again in a clash of club and machetes, nails and blades grinding together in front of the kitchen window. The tropical storm is growing even more powerful beyond the walls, a strong gust of wind ripping at the wooden shutters and tearing them clean from the window. Edgar and Jack jostle for position as the wind literally blows the window inward, little pieces of shattered glass flying against struggling faces. A torrent of rain blows in and sprays against Edgar and Jack, the water running across gritted teeth and straining musculature.

Edgar manages to bring the handle of the club up and smash Jack in the side of the face, knocking him away from the window and into a rack filled with porcelain plates. One of Jack's machetes slips from his hand and clatters somewhere under the kitchen counter, leaving the demon-infused boy with only a single blade to utilize.

There's the sound of splintering wood as trees get uprooted in the storm raging outside, lightning flashing across the sky and sending blinding light into the confines of the kitchen. Jack rises with the lightning still shining in his eyes, a solitary machete held tightly in his right hand.

Edgar charges again like a mad bull, all shaking rolls of flesh and deranged fury. Jack catches the first swing of the club and deflects it with the machete, but the next blow from the spiked head catches Jack directly in his Kevlar-protected chest. The boy flies backwards and smashes up against the door of the pantry, all the wind knocked out of him. He crumples downward into a sitting position against the door, coughing and choking in an effort to get oxygen back into his lungs.

Edgar shambles closer, a gurgling chuckle coming from behind the leather of his mask. He sounds like a man who knows that he has won. The thunder mingles with his laughter, loud crashes that rattle House Malencourt, the lights flickering and adding to the shadows. Jack's cheek is pressed against the pantry door, the boy still struggling to get his breath back.

Edgar raises the club up over his head in both hands, his intended target Jack's skull...

Suddenly Jack's eyes go fully black, the irises lost in fathomless darkness as Verminort assumes full control. Those black gulfs fall upon Edgar, and from the lips of a boy the demon whispers a fateful summoning.

"Pestilence...fall upon him."

Jack's finger points directly at Malencourt...and then they come. They come from beneath the floorboards, from holes and cracks in the walls and ceiling, from the broken window above the sink...from all entry points they come.

Hundreds of rats, some plump and large, others young and small...scurrying across the floor to crawl up Edgar's pants, to leap from the counter onto his chest and shoulders, the rodents falling upon Malencourt like he's the biggest wheel of cheese they've ever seen.

The rodents bite and tear at the fat man with their sharp little teeth, forcing him to lose his concentration and panic, spinning around erratically as he beats at his own body. The rats hang from sagging skin like corrupted jewelry, tails swishing and fangs buried and awash with blood. Edgar stumbles against the pantry door, the rat suit growing across his body, his meaty fists smashing down and instantly killing many of Verminort's little rodent soldiers.

Jack rises while Edgar is distracted, the boy panting and full of fresh adrenaline. Jack sprints forward as fast as he can and tackles the giant, the two of them smashing into the pantry door. The door is knocked clean off the hinges and both of them crash forward into the pantry, rolling around on the ground beneath the many shelves above. The machete and the club were dropped in the scuffle, both weapons lying strewn across the floor right along with the combatants themselves.

Edgar stirs, many of the rats crushed to death beneath his weight. Jack is the first to gain his footing, his head shaking from side to side to drive the cobwebs out. Jack's eyes open wide and his jaw unhinges at the sight of the inhuman display surrounding him. The formaldehyde from the many jars casts a sickly green illumination across his face. He spins in a slow circle, taking in the little horrors that all the jars contain. All these severed parts...all this bottled perversity.

Flashes of lost children filter through Jack's mind. The discarded clothing in the sewers, the little butterfly hair band, missing person posters plastered all over trees and utility poles in Greyfield.

Jack feels his anger rising anew, whirling and powerful like the storm tearing at the walls. The boy's eyes narrow, his gaze momentarily falling on Malencourt as he struggles up to his hands and knees.

"You sick, disgusting *MOTHERFUCKER*!"

Jack sends a HARD boot into Edgar's face, the steel toe flipping the fat man onto his back and right back down to the floor. Edgar gasps, proceeding to roll onto his side and spit a bloody tooth out of his plump, shredded lips.

Jack turns back to the shelves and the unspeakable collection of jars. He sights Edgar's club on the floor and he bends down to pick it up. The boy raises the spiked club up high...and he begins to smash it into the jars one by one, the glass shattering and formaldehyde splashing out across the floor.

An emotional roar flows from Jack's lips, tears streaming unknowingly down his cheeks as he destroys the horrible, sad secrets that Edgar has kept locked up in this little room for so very long. Chunks of the jars fly and the noxious liquid within splashes around the pantry, Jack fully lost in the moment.

He destroys the souvenirs of the monster of Greyfield. He destroys the little parts so callously taken from those that deserved to live long, happy lives. Jack smashes and he screams...and in this cramped little pantry with a demon lurking behind his soul, Jack destroys the last vestiges of his childhood.

Edgar has risen to his knees on the floor, the giant shaking with disbelief. His eyes are peeled wide open, his bleeding mouth pulled down into a wounded grimace. Half the leather mask has been ripped clean off his face, exposing puffy, infected flesh. The fat man's fists clench, a little squelch sound coming from his blackened, rotting hand.

His voice rises in the pantry, a torn and haunted piping, a creature of tattered sanity and pure, irredeemable hatred.

"My collection...my collection...my *sweet treats*...YOU FUCKIN' DEVIL BRAT...WHAT HAVE YOU DONE!!!!"

Edgar sweeps a meaty forearm into Jack's leg and brings the boy crumbling down on his back. The fat man struggles to rise, pushing and scraping against broken shelves, his face fuming behind the torn remnants of the Anguish mask. He finally attains a shaky vertical base...and he lunges downward on top of Jack in an attempt to crush him beneath all his weight.

Jack's hand scrambles out at the last possible second and takes hold of the dropped machete, bringing it up in a single thrust as Edgar falls downward. There's a hideous slice sound as the blade punctures Malencourt's stomach, carbon fiber sliding past flesh and internal organs. A hot splash of blood gushes across Jack's upper chest as the big man's enormous weight collapses down on top of him.

The blade exits through Malencourt's back, the tip of it coated in viscera. Edgar's face contorts into a pained rictus, his bad hand scraping and clawing at the source of his impalement. Jack's vest is thoroughly wet now and blood has begun to spill from Edgar's parted lips, dripping down into Jack's upturned face. The boy struggles beneath the girth of the giant...but there's still fight left in the monster of Greyfield. That rotting, fetid hand reaches upwards—the fingers shaking with effort—to close around Jack's mouth and nose, clamping his airways shut.

Edgar bears down with the last of his fading strength, Jack's eyes bulging as he starts to suffocate.

A muddy whisper falls from Edgar's lips, blood bubbles starting to pop in his flared nostrils as he pushes down even harder in an effort to snuff out his adversary.

"Saved a spot...for you, devil boy. Right there on that top shelf..."

Edgar exhales his foul, blood-speckled breath into Jack's face, the thick sausage fingers squeezing hard against the boy's nose and mouth.

"I ain't letting Death's bony hand touch on me...until I've stuffed your broken bits into a...a...prize jar..."

Ragged coughs tear through Edgar's body, but still he lays into Jack, his big tombstone teeth coated in plasma and bared in a final grin.

Jack is fading fast, his eyelids fluttering as the darkness starts to creep in. He is vaguely aware of Verminort working his right hand, using it to search and seek across the floor of the pantry. The fingers close around something sharp and hard. Jack realizes immediately what it is...and his eyes open wide with newfound hope. He closes his little hand around a piece of shattered glass from one of Edgar's jars, and he jams it upwards as hard as he possibly can into Malencourt's exposed throat.

Edgar's face seems to ripple with surprise, his grip on Jack's lower face falling away. The boy takes advantage of that moment by *dragging* the piece of glass to the side, severing Edgar's jugular vein and allowing a spray of arterial blood to shoot out from the cut throat like red water from a demonic sprinkler.

There's a nasty gurgling sound as Edgar tries to breathe through the ruin that is his throat, and Jack and Verminort combine the remainder of their will to wiggle out from underneath the fat man and flip him over onto his back.

He lies there like a dying cockroach, limbs weakly flailing as the pool of blood grows and grows around his massive carcass.

All the light fades from Edgar Malencourt's piggish little eyes. The last breath he takes into his lungs is a wet whistle, blood continuing to leak out past the shard of jar that is embedded in his neck. He dies with his pantry of power destroyed, his *sweet treats* scattered and ruined all around him.

The legacy of Anguish dies with him.

There's a loud crack from the sky the moment Edgar passes from the world, lighting striking the house somewhere on the upper floor. The wind starts to die down, replaced by the sound of fresh flames sizzling somewhere on the second floor of House Malencourt.

Jack remains there for a moment, staring down into the face of Greyfield's fallen monster. He rises shakily up to his feet, his whole body aching from head to toe. He pauses only to spit up a glob of blood and phlegm into Edgar's face before staggering out of the pantry. Verminort's voice is a soft whisper in the boy's head.

"Time to go, Jack. Let the fire do the rest of the work."

The boy and his demon stumble towards the front door, the two of them emerging into the storm-ravaged night. They turn the body they share around in the yard and watch as the flames lick the old wood of House Malencourt, the inferno growing and spreading, turning the house's windows into burning eyes that seem to glare out with undying malice.

The fire consumes the nexus of evil that has scarred the town of Greyfield for so many long years.

And as the rain tapers off and the howling wind becomes nothing more than a cool breeze, the lightning-born fire cleanses. Jack watches, the firelight dancing in his eyes, one bright blue, the other obsidian black.

26

Jack 2.0

We sit and watch House Malencourt being eaten by the blaze. A huge oak tree was uprooted in the storm and the rough bark of the trunk makes a good seat for this fireworks show. There is destruction everywhere we look. Tree limbs scattered, Edgar's tow truck with a broken weathervane impaled through the windshield, little streams of muddy flood water turning the yard into a temporary swamp.

The fire burns brightly now, a beautiful kaleidoscope of reds and oranges and yellows. Sirens drone in the distance all over town but due to the widespread damage none of the emergency vehicles are aware of House Malencourt's fate just yet. Maybe it's just a mirage but at one point I think I see wispy phantoms drifting up out of the fire and into the sky where the dark clouds are finally parting. The phantoms look like the vague outline of children, all of Edgar's victims. I can even make out the look of gratitude etched across little ghostly faces as they float ever upward into the unknown.

I detect a slithery sensation from Verminort when he sights these same phantoms—something like agitation—but he makes no comment about their passing. I can't help but smile. The little souls kept locked away in Edgar's filthy jars deserve freedom and happiness in whatever waits beyond the walls of this world. I'm just glad I was able to obtain a measure of vengeance against the monster that locked them away in the first place.

As the fire dances there comes a mysterious cry from somewhere in one of the upper bedrooms. There doesn't seem to be much pain in this cry. It seems almost thankful...a sad sound of release. It's gone as soon as it begins.

"Who was that?"

"No one to worry about. The pitiful creature Edgar kept tied up in that bedroom welcomes death. Trust me, it's a mercy."

Verminort will say no more on the subject, little sections of House Malencourt starting to cave in as black smoke plumes higher into the atmosphere. A sense of finality hangs in the air. I feel as though an impossible task has been accomplished, the weight of untold horrors finally sliding from my young shoulders. After a long, strange trip through the darkest tunnel I have ever known, there is finally a twinkle of light at the end.

"Is it over, Verminort? *Really* over?"

My demon pauses, seeming to consider the question.

"It's over, Jack. The pact is fulfilled, the covenant is upheld. I promised to help you gain your revenge and destroy the man who nearly killed you. Edgar Malencourt is food for the fire now. Your tormenter is dead...and our deal is done."

I can't help but sigh in relief. I feel suddenly so very tired. I can't wait to take a shower and wash the layers of grime from my skin.

"Thank you, Verminort. This is the weirdest shit I've ever been through in my whole life...but I couldn't have done this without you."

"I aim to please, roomie..."

"So is this the part where you leave my body and return to Hell? I finally get to go home...I finally get to see my mom..."

There is no answer, only a growing sensation in my head. It feels like yet another storm gathering, but this one is confined to the limits of my skull. I can feel the swirling red and black cloud slithering and crawling through my thoughts and memories, closer and closer to that part of me where the soul resides.

"Not exactly."

Goosebumps break out across my arms as the fear spreads through me. Those two words shatter the sense of relief I was feeling just a few moments ago. My head feels suddenly very hot. There's a sensation of constriction...

"I've grown to like you, roomie. I really have. You're one tough cookie! I feel like we've kinda bonded, ya know? Most of the super famous demons like Abaddon and Beelzebub like to get into a body and just corrupt it, fuck it up from the inside out and ruin the meat-vehicle just because they can. It's an ego thing, I guess. Not the case for you and I, though. We've been all about teamwork. Batman and Robin ain't got shit on this dynamic duo!"

My head is hurting very badly now. It feels like the migraine of all migraines is building just behind my temples.

"But uhh...all that aside, I'm gonna have to evict you, roomie. Every demon's greatest wish is to find and secure flesh, and I've done that. This body is pretty freakin' awesome, and I've got some redecorations planned. I had no problems sharing it with you during the course of our deal, but now that the deal is done, it's time for you to get the fuck out, Jackie boy."

I press my hands against my temples, my teeth gritted against the throbbing pain in my skull.

"You...you...said you would leave...you said you'd give my body back to me..."

"Newsflash, Jack: I'm a demon. Demons are evil. Demons lie. Trusting a demon is like handing a gangbanger your keys and asking him to watch your car for you. Not the best idea, kiddo..."

I try to respond but a flash of pain splits through my skull, forcing me down to my hands and knees with a scream echoing out past my lips. It feels like there's acid in my brain and everything is being corroded.

"Let me walk you through what happens now. We're taking a little trip inside of your mind, Jack. The place where your soul and my essence currently reside. It's a painful trip, as you can probably attest right now. When we get there...make this easy on yourself. Take your fluttery little moth of a soul and kindly vacate the premises. Because if you fight me, Jack...I'm gonna have to boot you out. That will be very unpleasant for you."

I've fallen onto my back, my entire body starting to convulse. My eyes have rolled up to the whites and I can't see anything. I taste little bits of froth oozing from the corners of my mouth.

I feel myself flying away from my body, deeper and deeper into the core of my own mind. I'm already resisting, gritting my teeth and trying to escape the tornado of the black and red cloud that's enveloping me.

"Seriously, Jack? You're already struggling? Alright. We'll do it the hard way. I'm fixing to open up a whole case of demonic whupass on you..."

I see nothing but the swirling black and red cloud, the particles slithering and crawling all around me. I'm falling...and finally I hit some hard surface, the wind knocked out of me as the red and black cloud starts to drift away.

27

Jack (The House That Is My Skull)

The cloud withdraws, tendrils of black and red particles seeming to caress my body like heated fingers as it goes. I'm finally able to get some air back into my lungs and I sit up, taking a moment to gaze at my surreal surroundings. I'm lying on the surface of some black and blasted wasteland, a floating island of obsidian land that seems to be only about a mile across on each side. I realize immediately that this is some sort of arena that Verminort has created in my mind, a place made for a reckoning.

The blasted obsidian island seems to just hang in fathomless space; two giant stars somewhere far up in a blackened sky. The stars seem to be flashing with pictures of the outside world and the vaguest image of House Malencourt burning. It startles me to realize that the stars are my eyes seen from the confines of my own skull, staring out at the world beyond this arena of the mind.

There are great shimmering spheres floating through the air all around me, seeming like large bubbles passing slowly by. The surfaces of the spheres are reflective and translucent, and as one floats dangerously close to me my gaze is pulled to the scene playing within the sphere. It's a memory. It's a recollection from my early childhood, me and mom tubing along the peaceful waters of the Potomac River. The sun felt so warm on my skin that day and life felt full of possibilities.

The memory sphere drifts away and off into the abyss, and I make out the memories contained within so many others that are floating casually by. There's me at ten years old sitting at my school desk and listening to the oldest man in town—Abel Campbell—tell stories about his life to bright-eyed students. There's a glimpse of my puppy Shoggoth chasing his tail in another sphere. There's me and my friend Dave staring into my terrarium and watching my toads gobble up crickets. Every single moment of my life is contained in these shimmering bubbles, the memory spheres floating all around me like dandelion seeds caught in a breeze.

From across the blasted landscape of jagged obsidian a form walks towards me. It's the black and red cloud, swirled into a rudimentary outline of a body. A tall, lithe body constantly distorted by motion. The briefest glimpse of inky rodent-like eyes appear set within the head of the cloud, only to be swept away by the constant swirling of the disembodied entity.

The tall form stops a few yards away from me, seeming to stare directly at me with eyeless determination. The memory spheres float all around it, totally ignored as they pass the bodiless entity.

"Welcome to the House That Is Your Skull, Jack. Pretty sweet view, huh?"

Verminort's voice is unmistakable, the voice of an accuser, seducer, deceiver. It's almost pleasant to the ears even now.

I stare across the blasted lands at the demon's bodiless form, my fists clenching at my sides.

"Hope you like what I've done with the place..."

"Get out of my head. Our deal is done...and now I want you to leave."

"Rude! Without me you'd be a corpse covered in sewer worms right now, you ungrateful little brat. I saved you. I lead you to your vengeance. You got what you wanted. Now...it's time that I get what I want..."

"You did save me. You also deceived me. This has been all about your quest for a body since the moment you made that deal with me..."

"Can't argue that. I've been shopping around for a nice flesh suit for ages now. Just so happens there was naive, dying boy willing to let me step into the dressing room and try his on for size."

The tall, distorted form is swirling even more now, seeming to prepare for a lunge.

"Yours is the perfect fit, Jack."

All talk ceases as Verminort speeds forward and smashes into me, knocking me back down to the blasted surface of the ground. The demon's speed is uncanny, almost invisible to the naked eye. My hands fly up in my face as I fall and I take time to notice that they're ghostly and white, seeming to give off little auras of wispy mist. I'm not struggling against Verminort with my physical body. I'm struggling against him with my soul...

Before I can even attempt to rise my ankle is clamped by Verminort's swirling hand, the heat of it making me gasp. It's like feeling a soul-burn, something that goes even deeper than bone. The demon begins to drag me across the surface of this blasted island of the mind, my soul bumping and scraping against the jagged obsidian. We're getting closer and closer to the edge of the island, a fluttery panic alighting deep within me. Somewhere in the recesses of my unexplored subconscious I understand that if Verminort casts me over the edge of the blasted island, my soul will be lost to the purgatory that lies between life and death. The demon will have full control of my body after that and he'll be able to do whatever he pleases with it.

If I go over the edge, Verminort wins.

I'm clawing and grasping at the jagged obsidian, but I can't seem to get a handhold. Verminort just keeps on dragging me, the demon actually whistling and taking his time with getting me to the place where the blasted land drops off into sheer nothingness.

"Shame it has to go down like this, Jack. It might give you some peace to know that I'm gonna really enjoy this body of yours once it's fully mine. I'm probably gonna spend my childhood getting into lots of fist fights in elementary school, definitely gonna fuck a bunch of sluts in high school, probably gonna experiment with some hard drugs way before I hit the age of eighteen, too. Definitely gonna make the most of this flesh."

I'm desperate now, my fingers scrabbling hard against the torn and blasted obsidian. I manage to grip a piece of the volcanic glass but Verminort gives a hard pull on my ankle and it breaks off in my hand.

"And after I turn eighteen? That's when the fun REALLY begins! Stabbings, shootings, jaywalking...gonna try pretty much every violent crime once or twice. I'm definitely gonna

devote a few years to a pyromania phase. Burning entire cities to the ground just sounds too good to pass up!"

We're at the edge now, only endless blackness waiting on the other side. Verminort picks me up by the scruff of the neck, his grip hot and preternaturally strong. I try to fight out of it, but my soul is drained after the fight with Malencourt. It feels like I have nothing left.

"Guess this is goodbye. It's been one hell of a ride, Jack. We've laughed together. We've killed together. We've eaten rats together. Kinda feels like I'm losing my best friend."

Verminort pulls me backward by the neck, preparing to throw me off the edge and into the purgatory that lies beyond. I struggle in vain, pawing and scratching at his hot, intangible grip. It's no good. I'm at the demon's mercy now.

The swirling, cloudy form leans close to my face, and I can almost make out a ratty grin spreading beneath the whirling particles of red and black.

"Luckily for me, demons aren't all that sentimental. Happy trails, roomie!"

Verminort tightens his grip and starts to hurl me forward...but something stops him from completing the throw. It's a strange, hollow popping sound. I look down, puzzling over the sight standing before us. It's a little phantom of a boy, seeming to have popped out of thin air. His face is grim, his eyes glaring at Verminort. He has a little Ghostbusters lunchbox with the name "Billy" written across it in magic marker.

That hollow pop sound comes again, and another ghostly child stands next to Billy. This one is a cute little girl with a butterfly hair band. It's the exact same hair band I found floating in the sewer not so long ago...

Her eyes are fixed and intense, that same glare falling upon the demon known as Verminort. More pops, more children. I see two with similar facial features, obviously twins. That hollow little sound keeps coming, and more phantom children keep popping into existence. Verminort seems almost to twitch each time he hears this ominous sound.

A whole pack of wispy white children stand before us now, their clothes in all manner of bedraggled state. They are deathly silent, all those little dead eyes staring holes into the swirling form of Verminort. I recognize them now. They're the same little phantoms that floated skyward as House Malencourt burned to the ground.

They're all of Edgar's little victims, small souls finally freed from the twisted incarceration of many haunting glass jars.

"No..."

Verminort tries hard to mask the fear in his voice, but he fails.

"I cannot be cast out...not when I'm this close...no..."

The little phantoms are moving now, crowding forward and driving Verminort back. They circle him and drive him close to the edge of the blasted land, the demon's swirling feet coming dangerously close to the edge. The twins reach down to where I'm lying and pick me up by the arms, their hands feeling nice and cold against my soul-skin. I'm standing with the horde of ghostly children now. We stand together against Verminort, many sets of eyes marking the demon with quiet contempt.

He stands there, trying hard to balance on the edge...and all of us rush forward towards the demon. It's like a little pack of hyenas using the numbers game against a more powerful lion, many ghostly hands pushing and beating against the swirling form of Verminort. He fights hard for a moment, trying to regain his footing, but it soon becomes too late. I reach forward with my little phantom saviors and deliver a final great push to the clouded chest of the demon, sending him flying off the edge and into the oblivion below.

A final, defiant roar echoes up as he falls.

"NO...FUCKIN'...FAIR!!!"

I can just make out two swirling demonic hands throwing up middle fingers at us before Verminort vanishes into the endless darkness of the beyond.

I collapse downward after that, the little phantoms starting to gather around me and crouch down closer. The true relief sinks in now as all those little ghostly faces look down upon me with kind eyes. I'm able to articulate a small whisper in response.

"Thank you."

Billy smiles, offering me a little nod. The boy then reaches down and places a gentle, cold hand across my chest. The other little phantoms follow his lead, many tiny hands landing across my soul-flesh just above the heart. I see the eyes of the children closing, almost like they're concentrating very hard on something.

I remember only a blast of white light after that as this arena of the mind fades away.

28

Jack

The first thing I'm aware of upon waking is the acrid stench of smoke caught by the wind. My eyes open to the night sky, distant and familiar constellations setting my mind at ease. I'm back in the real world, the rubble of House Malencourt little more than a smoking, crumbled foundation now. I roll over onto my side, simply lying there for a moment and gazing at the remnants of Edgar's den. I'm listening to my own thoughts. I'm concentrating very hard on hearing that blabbermouth chattering of Verminort's voice in my head, hoping against all hopes that I don't hear it. Seconds turn into minutes...and my thoughts remain my own.

The demon is gone, his presence extinguished from my mind and my body. A radiant smile breaks out across my face, and I can't help but send up a triumphant whoop into the smoky night sky. It feels amazing to be free of Verminort, his infernal claws withdrawn from everything that I am. I know in my heart the phantom children had the biggest role in exorcising the demon possessing me, and for that I'll never forget each and every one of them. I owe those little lost ones my life.

I stumble up to my feet, brushing leaves and dirt from my already filthy clothes. The scene has changed very little since the convulsions sent me into that arena of the mind, the only difference now the total collapse of House Malencourt. I don't bother giving that hideous place even a second glance.

I have more important things on my mind. I'm thinking about a destination that I've longed for ever since Edgar abducted me at the edge of the bog seemingly a lifetime ago. It's a place that has lived in my heart, giving me the strength and the resolve to weather every kind of storm that has come my way. In the depths of the sewer it gave me hope, and in the fight for my life against the monster of Greyfield I kept telling myself that I can't die without going back there at least one last time. It's been my constant, my distant glowing lantern in a night that seems to last forever.

I'm thinking about home.

That's where I'm going now, staggering and limping past the downed trees and splintered utility poles that litter Edgar's driveway. I slip safely into the woods across the road just as several fire trucks cruise into view, flashing lights painting the night and sirens blaring in the storm-torn silence.

***

The sun is creeping over the horizon as I stumble along my street, every corner familiar, every house along the way etched so beautifully into my memory. The storm's destructive path is visible everywhere, tree limbs lying across the sidewalks, a fire hydrant busted and spraying water into the air, even a random doghouse blown from someone's yard by the wind and smashed against the asphalt. I weave between these obstructions like a particularly tired zombie, the little brown cottage I'm seeking akin to a perfect mirage glimmering in the newly risen sun. It's a humble, quaint little house. At this particular moment in life, it looks like the most jaw-dropping mansion I've ever seen.

I hear the shrill little bark of a Yorkshire terrier and the tears start falling shamelessly down my cheeks. My little dog Shoggoth races out from behind a section of ravaged hedge and meets me on the walkway leading to my front door. I fall to my knees, burying my face in the fur of the little animal. It smells wonderful. It smells like home. Shoggoth licks my cheeks, lapping up the tears and dancing around me in excited little circles.

There's a figure there in the doorway. She was holding a broom in her hands but the moment she sees me the broom falls to the ground, totally forgotten. My mom's mouth is unhinged, her eyes as wide as saucers. The sunlight twinkles across cheekbones that are just as wet with tears as my own. She stands there a moment staring at me, frozen in disbelief.

"Hi, mom."

Those two words are all it takes to break her paralysis, the hug that envelopes me so fierce and full of emotion. Her hands grip at my dirty clothes, her fingers running through my greasy hair. I return the hug, my arms wrapping around her as I allow my head to fall against her shoulder. Everything feels right now. The whole world seems bright and good when you finally make it home.

After a long moment she reluctantly releases me, her hands still tight against my shoulders, almost like she fears if she lets me go I'll vanish off into the unknown again.

"Where have you been, Jack?"

I can't help but smile. I fall willingly back into the hug, Shoggoth dancing around our entangled feet as the sun fully dawns on the little town of Greyfield.

"To Hell and back, mom."

It doesn't seem enough to say it once, so I repeat the phrase, another little chuckle escaping my lips.

"To Hell and back."

I glance up at the sky, taking in the incredible vista of blue and fluffy white. All of the dark storm clouds have passed now.

Greyfield even feels different. It feels unburdened. It feels safe...

"And now that I'm back...I could really use a shower."

29

The Pit

Edgar Malencourt opens his bleary eyes to unfamiliar, alien surroundings. He has the worst headache of his lifetime, his skull feeling like it's been split wide open with a jackhammer. His vision seems smeared and reddish, his eyeballs feeling terribly dry within the sockets. He cannot blink, some sort of nameless instrument peeling his eyelids back and denying him the luxury of closing his eyes. He tries to look around, little razorblades of pain slicing through his neck each time he turns in a new direction. He sees only distant glass walls and the blurry, flickering images of some nightmare world beyond the glass. He is confused...and for the first time in ages, the monster of Greyfield is afraid. None of this makes sense.

There is the vaguest memory of blood and ravaged flesh lurking in the center of his thoughts. He doesn't know how he got here. He doesn't even know where *here* is. Wasn't there a boy? Wasn't there a battle? It all seems faded and forgotten. This must be a dream. There are jagged screams and someone is playing a pipe organ beyond the glass. The sounds mix into macabre music. Edgar tries to lift up his hands to cover his eardrums but his arms are bound to something that feels like warm metal. Everything feels wrong.

There's the creaking of rusty wheel spokes nearing the place where Edgar is bound. A very large antique wheelchair appears in front of Malencourt, the occupant of that wheelchair forcing a low, pathetic moan to fall from the lips of the man who once wore the Anguish mask.

Sue is naked and filthy, a grinning mound of defiled blubber that stares into the very depths of Edgar's soul with idiotic intensity. The secret sister is sucking greedily on a red lollipop, the ooze from it splattering past her plump lips and running over her rolls of flab like little streams of freshly drawn blood. She waves the stumps of her amputated arms at Edgar, actually managing to clap her stumps together like a child full of excitement. Edgar wishes so very desperately that he could close his eyes. He can smell his sister, the disgusting aroma stinging his nostrils and forcing tears out of the corners of his eyes. She is the embodiment of decay, all festering bedsores and unwashed meat. The wheelchair moves ever closer, seemingly by Sue's sheer willpower, the scarred stumps of her legs kicking in girlish glee mere inches from Edgar's own.

It's at this moment that Edgar realizes he's dead. With his sister's giant moon of a face inches from his own—her braying donkey-like laughter sending bolts of pain through his head and splatters of lollipop ooze into his eyes—he understands the true hopelessness of his situation. He is dead...and this is Hell.

The moment this realization sinks in a transformation passes through the mountainous fat of Sue, her body contorting and reshaping itself, bones cracking and flesh tearing, the image of his unfortunate sister vanishing into the new form. The metamorphosis complete, Edgar can only gape at the figure seated in the wheelchair. Verminort seems not to notice, the demon crossing his legs casually while making eye contact with his victim.

Verminort is a sight to behold in his native habitat. The demon wears a finely tailored suit that conforms perfectly to his tall, lithe form. The suit is stitched together from human flesh and dyed the deepest scarlet, soaked to the fullest red in the blood of all those Verminort has had the honor of torturing during his tenure in the thirteenth circle. He has the head of a rat, his fur very dark and his inky eyes showing nothing but lifelessness. He regards Edgar with a little grin, his lips pulling backward to expose rows of sharp, crooked teeth that are stained a murky yellow.

Edgar shivers with fear at the sight of this living pestilence, his neck shaking from side to side, but his gaze is fixed and he's unable to turn away from the demon in the wheelchair. Just the sight of Verminort makes Edgar's stomach start to hurt, his intestines feeling like they're caving inward and slithering around inside of him like agitated serpents.

"I was so damn close, Edgar. Closer than I've ever been. I finally had a body on the Earthly plane. A meat-vehicle all my own...flesh to play with."

The demon sounds wistful, his voice echoing in this strange glass cave. Edgar starts to blubber, repeating the words "no" and "please" at random intervals. Verminort ignores these little utterances.

"It's a real bummer when your dreams come crashing down like that. Kinda takes the wind outta your sails..."

Verminort sighs, proceeding to rise up out of the wheelchair and walk towards one of the glass walls. He places a hand with sharp little talons against the glass, staring out at the desolate Hellscape that is the thirteenth circle. There on the horizon is the broken, charnel city of Nis, black and monolithic structures reaching towards the overcast sky like fingers breaking through the soil of a lonely grave. The putrid waters of the river Styx pass much closer to the glass wall, a sluggish snake carrying bloated corpses along the current with the stench of human waste wafting up from the rippling surface. There's a giant barren willow tree on the riverbank, the limbs deformed and devoid of all leaves, the roots nourished by the foul juices that feed into the current of Styx.

Many decapitated heads hang from the limbs of the tree, affixed there with lengths of rusty chain, the rotten, vacant faces blowing lightly in a bone-dust breeze. There's a young woman there beneath the tree, digging and carving at the ruinous bark with something that looks like a straight razor. She wears all black, her mane of midnight hair blowing out wildly across her shoulders. She suddenly stops, stepping back from her work while turning to catch Verminort's gaze. A huge smile crosses the girl's pale, pixielike face...and she offers Verminort a little wave of black nail polished fingers.

The carving on the tree reads "ROSE & RO 4EVER".

Verminort offers Thorny Rose a little halfhearted wave in return, proceeding to turn from the glass and place his full attention on Edgar once again.

"Guess I'll have to settle for playing with your flesh, big fella."

Edgar's belly hurts worse than ever now. It's a sickening throb of pain that makes sweat burst from the pores along his forehead and drip down to the very tip of his nose. He tries very hard to crane his neck downward, and he succeeds just a little, getting his very first look at his own body. His eyes widen. His mouth falls open and the bleakest sound falls out, horror and revulsion mingling together to hop off his tongue and bounce off the glass walls surrounding him.

His stomach is a torn, shredded crater. The flesh has been flayed back, exposing blood-soaked viscera and quivering mounds of internal guts. But the worst thing of all? There are hundreds of multi-colored lollipops shoved down into the bleeding hole of Edgar's belly. He flops from side to side in the chair, the binding cutting deeply into his wrists.

Verminort watches this, the expression that crosses his rodent face seeming deeply amused. He raises up one black paw and snaps his fingers together. The rats answer the demon's call, the scurrying little critters emerging from the shadows and all racing towards the bleeding wound that is Edgar's stomach. They leap up onto the chair and crawl across Edgar's thighs, entering into the wound and beginning to chow down on intestines and lollipops alike. The little rat army just keeps on coming, seemingly endless, piling into the fat man's gut-hole and eating and eating and eating...

Edgar Malencourt's screams are legendary. They rise into entirely new spectrums of sound, the vocal cords rupturing inside his throat. On the zero to ten pain scale, he's experiencing something far beyond a ten. He's feeling excruciation that stretches into the realm of infinity...

Verminort turns away, seeming suddenly bored. He returns to the glass and looks outward, listening to the peaceful sounds of the rats munching on meat and Edgar screaming for mercy that will never reach him.

"Take your time with this feast, my brethren. We only have eternity..."

The voice of the demon is answered by many greedy squeaks and renewed gnawing.

"Welcome home, Edgar Malencourt."

The view fades outward and upward, encompassing the entire panorama of the glass structure that Edgar and Verminort now reside in. It's a giant jar wedged into the center of a dead volcano. It seems here in the Pit...Edgar is the *sweetest treat* of all.

"Welcome home..."

January 28th 2015- April 7th 2015

Jeremy Megargee

Afterword

What a long, strange trip it's been...

I want to take a minute to personally thank my readers for coming along with me on this trip. I'm not sure where any story is going to take me until I actually sit down in front of the keyboard. I'm the type of writer that doesn't spend hours storyboarding and detailing every single plot point, that's just not how my process works. I'm a writer that basically "flies by the seat of his pants"...as Stephen King puts it.

I get ideas and I allow those ideas to fit together into my head like puzzle pieces until they resemble something like the skeleton of a story. It then becomes my job to cover that skeleton in flesh and attempt to make it dance. That's my creative process, and it's always a great deal of fun for me.

I can honestly say that I don't feel in control of the characters or the plot of any story that I write. I feel as though I'm just the vessel through which the words flow and the characters basically do the work for me in telling the tale and creating the atmosphere of their own little fictional worlds.

I had a few ideas floating around in my head for my second novel, but *Sweet Treats* just felt like the *right* novel to write at this particular time in my life. It's a short little revenge tale full of characters that made me feel a whole different range of emotions. I enjoyed writing from Jack's perspective, just a good kid who got involved in some really deep shit. Verminort was a favorite too; I really had fun playing around with the concept of a chatty demon with a sense of humor. I didn't enjoy writing Edgar at all, honestly started to hate him about halfway through the novel. He's just a vile and repulsive individual—which makes him the perfect antagonist—and even as the author I was rooting for Jack and Verminort to take the rotten bastard down in the end.

For me this book felt like a chance to refine my craft a bit more and really develop a unique voice as a writer. I consider *Dirt Lullabies* my practice novel (don't get me wrong, I feel very strongly about that book and I love the characters) but it was my first novel and I was still learning the whole self-publishing process and trying to get it down to a science. I think I've come a long way with book formatting and improving the readability of my stories, but as human beings we never stop learning and attempting to improve, so I'll continue to strive to make my books better with every single release moving forward from here.

All writers grow and evolve with time, and as long as I've got people out there who are interested in the words I put on blank pages, I'll keep writing...because you should never stop doing something that you love.

ABOUT THE AUTHOR:

When I was still a child and picked up my very first Goosebumps book by R. L. Stine, I knew I'd fallen head over heels in love with all things horror. It's a love affair that has only grown stronger over the years, a borderline obsession with stories that explore the darkest recesses of the human imagination. I guess you could say I'm like Thorny Rose in that way...always stalking down those special stories that have the ability to invoke a creepy-crawly feeling right down in the marrow of my bones.

As I grew older I discovered the work of some of my biggest inspirations like Stephen King, Edgar Allan Poe, H.P. Lovecraft, Clive Barker...and the work of those authors sent me deeper down the path of the macabre. During my teenage years I had the little tradition of reading Stephen King's The Stand each summer to lose myself in the devastation of the superflu and marvel at the sadistic magnetism of Randall Flagg.

I've devoured horror fiction for as long as I can remember and reading the words weaved by the greats of the genre inspired me to begin writing. I wanted the opportunity to tell my own tales with the intent to terrify, to disturb; to capture the morbid curiosity of the reader just as my own was caught so early on in life.

If I've managed to inspire some of those feelings in you, my readers, then I feel that I've accomplished something just a little bit magical. There's still some magic left in this world, and I think it's most powerful when manifested in the form of words scrawled across many blank pages. Granted any magic contained within my work will be of the dark variety...but I wouldn't want it any other way. ;)

Jeremy Megargee lives in Martinsburg, West Virginia with his little old pug Cerberus. When he's not writing, he enjoys hiking mountain trails, weight training, getting tattooed and being a garden variety introvert in his mid-20s. Oh, and reading too (duh).

Megargee is also the author of DIRT LULLABIES.

Connect with me online:

Facebook: www.facebook.com/JMHorrorFiction

Instagram: @xbadmoonrising

Thanks for reading!

<u>**What did you think of SWEET TREATS?**</u>

Feedback is incredibly important for indie authors. Most indie authors are not affiliated with Big Publishing and we don't have the vast resources or marketing tools to get our names out there compared to many of the advertised best-selling titles. Reviews give my work additional exposure and help new readers to discover my particular brand of horror.

If you enjoyed this book, I would love it if you could head over to the Amazon.com page for Sweet Treats and leave an honest review about what you thought of the story. I read every single review I get and I'm very grateful for the support.

Feel free to share this book with friends, word of mouth advertising goes a long way...and it helps the horror spread. ;)

CPSIA information can be obtained
at www.ICGtesting.com
Printed in the USA
LVHW081327240521
688333LV00022B/771